Ben's breath stirred the tendrils of hair hanging loose from her ponytail.

Kate leaned her back against the solid wall of muscles that was her bodyguard cowboy. The warmth of his arms around her reassured and scared her all at once.

Her hands shook so badly, she thought she might drop the gun.

"Are you afraid?" he whispered.

Yes, yes, she was afraid. Afraid of falling in love with a stranger. Afraid of investing her emotions in someone who would leave as soon as the threat was neutralized. Afraid she would be heartbroken when the dust settled on the Flying K Ranch.

ELLE JAMES

TRIGGERED

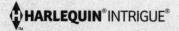

This book is dedicated to cowboys of all shapes, sizes and sexes. These brave men and women work hard, play hard and have a sense of loyalty, decency and ethics we should all aspire to.

ISBN-13: 978-0-373-69700-7

TRIGGERED

Recycling programs
for this product may
not exist in your area.

Printed in U.S.A.

™ www.Harlequin.com

ABOUT THE AUTHOR

A Golden Heart Award winner for Best Paranormal Romance in 2004, Elle James started writing when her sister issued a Y2K challenge to write a romance novel. She has managed a full-time job and raised three wonderful children, and she and her husband even tried their hands at ranching exotic birds (ostriches, emus and rheas) in the Texas Hill Country. Ask her, and she'll tell you what it's like to go toe-to-toe with an angry 350-pound bird! After leaving her successful career in information technology management, Elle is now pursuing her writing full-time. Elle loves to hear from fans. You can contact her at ellejames@earthlink.net or visit her website at www.ellejames.com.

Books by Elle James

HARLEQUIN INTRIGUE

938—DAKOTA MELTDOWN
961—LAKOTA BABY
987—COWBOY SANCTUARY
1014—BLOWN AWAY
1033—ALASKAN FANTASY
1052—TEXAS-SIZED SECRETS
1080—UNDER SUSPICION, WITH CHILD
1100—NICK OF TIME
1127—BABY BLING
1156—AN UNEXPECTED CLUE
1172—OPERATION XOXO
1191—KILLER BODY
1226—BUNDLE OF TROUBLE
1244—HOSTAGE TO THUNDER HORSE
1281—COWBOY BRIGADE
1306—ENGAGED WITH THE BOSS
1357—THUNDER HORSE HERITAGE
1382—THUNDER HORSE REDEMPTION
1433—TRIGGERED*

*Covert Cowboys, Inc.

HARLEQUIN NOCTURNE

147—THE WITCH'S INITIATION

CAST OF CHARACTERS

Ben Harding—Former cop in the Austin Police Department, now hired as a private investigator.

Kate Langsdon—Inherited the Flying K Ranch from the father she'd never known. Her husband killed in Afghanistan a month before their daughter was born. She is just looking to provide a safe home for her little girl.

Hank Winchester—Billionaire willing to take the fight for justice into his own hands by setting up CCI—Covert Cowboys, Inc.

Sheriff Fulmer—Sheriff of Wild Oak Canyon and surrounding county. He's the only law in the area.

Deputy Dwayne Schillinger—He works for Fulmer in the sheriff's department—and has an attitude.

Guillermo "Snake" Ramirez—Leader of local biker gang. Terror for hire to the highest bidder.

Cara Jo Smithson—Pretty single woman who owns the diner in Wild Oak Canyon.

Lily Langsdon—Kate's four-year-old daughter. She loves animals and playing outside.

Kyle Kendrick—The father Kate never knew.

Chapter One

Necessity, burning curiosity and a Hummer limo brought him here, but as Ben Harding sat in the leather armchair surrounded by three other men, he wondered what the heck he'd gotten himself into. He glanced around the room again. The only thing he had in common with the others was that they each wore a cowboy hat, jeans and boots.

Beyond that, he knew nothing about the men gathered in billionaire Hank Derringer's home. The Raging Bull Ranch lay in the heart of the back of beyond, South Texas, where men were tough, the drug runners were tougher and a property owner stood a good chance of getting killed riding across his own spread.

Ben had done his homework. Hank Derringer had become a recluse since he'd lost his family over a year ago in a botched kidnapping attempt. The man had made billions and continued to make more in the oil and gas industry. All facts that were easy enough to find. But why bring these men here? Why now?

Ben would have blown off the invitation to come if he'd had any other choice. His career at the Austin Police Department at an end, he'd been pounding the pavement looking for work and finding that no one, until now, wanted to hire a man who'd been kicked off the force for killing a man with his bare hands.

Did he regret what he'd done?

No.

And he'd do it again, given the same circumstances.

His gut clenched and he fought to push the rage and lingering images to the back of his mind as a tall, slightly older man joined them.

He wore a black Stetson and looked very much like the other men seated around the room. "Gentlemen, I'm Hank Derringer. Thank you all for coming to the Raging Bull Ranch." He sat near the huge stone fireplace, facing them. "I brought you here because you are the best of the best."

"Best of the best what, Hank?" The muscle-bound, blond-haired man across from Ben spoke first. He nodded toward Ben and the other two men. "And who are these guys?"

Hank tipped his head toward the man questioning him. "Patience, Thorn. I'm getting to that. For the rest of you, meet Thorn Drennan, the best sheriff Wild Oak Canyon ever had. A man the people could count on to fight for truth and justice."

Thorn's eyes narrowed. "You're forgetting—I'm no longer the sheriff."

"Precisely." Hank turned to the man with brown hair, brown eyes and a wicked scar across his right cheek. "Chuck Bolton. Your friends call you Big Tex, born and raised on a ranch near Amarillo. You know how to ride, rope and build fences like the best of them. Served two tours in Iraq and one in Afghanistan where you wiped out an entire Taliban stronghold against your commander's orders."

The man sat up straighter, his broad shoulders straining against the seams of his chambray shirt. "Got the boot and a bum leg for that."

"A man with courage and determination to fight the good fight," Hank said.

Big Tex shrugged. "I guess it depends on your definition of 'the good fight.'"

Hank moved on to the next person, a man sitting back from the rest, dark circles beneath his eyes, an intense, haunted expression in his green eyes as he stared out the window. "Special Agent Zachary Adams, one of the FBI's best undercover operatives working to stop the drug cartels along the border. Got caught in a bad situation on the wrong side of the border. Yet you survived."

"For what it was worth." The man's gaze shifted from the window to Hank. "And, just for the record, former FBI. I quit."

Hank nodded. "Right."

Derringer turned to Ben, his smile warm, welcoming. "And then there's Ben Harding, the most highly decorated officer on the Austin police force."

"*The* Ben Harding?" Big Tex snorted. "Weren't you the guy who was fired for strangling Frank Davis to death with your bare hands?"

Ben stiffened. He'd seen what the high-powered CEO had done to that young girl in a run-down warehouse on the seedier side of Austin. He'd watched him run from the scene of the crime with the child's blood on his hands and clothing. Ben hadn't cared who he was or what big company he ran. All he cared about was making the man pay for what he'd done to the girl.

Ben's stomach roiled as he recalled the scene and the memories of another very similar crime involving the deaths of his wife and young daughter.

His fingers balled into fists and he rose halfway out of his seat, ready to take on the world. "Yeah, I killed a man, what's it to you?"

Big Tex shrugged. "Just wondering."

"I read about it. Davis was a sick bastard into hurting little girls. I'd have done the same," the man called Zach said.

"You gave him what he deserved," Thorn agreed. "Why

waste money on a system that would have turned him loose to do it again?"

The starch taken out of his fight, Ben sat back against the soft brown leather of the wingback chair. He was disappointed he wouldn't have a brawl to release all the tension balled up in his gut since he'd arrived. At least now he felt more of a kinship with the others in the room.

Hank's mouth twisted into a wry grin. "You are all highly trained in your fields, and because of your various circumstances find yourselves unemployed."

Ben snorted. "Unemployable."

"Wrong." Hank's lips spread into a smile. "I'm here to offer you a position in a start-up corporation."

"Doing what? Sweeping floors? Who wants a bunch of rejects?" Zach asked.

"I need you." Hank rose from his chair. "Because you aren't rejects, you're just the type of men I'm looking for. Men who will fight for what you believe in, who were born or raised on a ranch, with the ethics and strength of character of a good cowboy. I'm inviting you to become a part of CCI, known only to those on the inside as Covert Cowboys, Inc., a specialized team of citizen soldiers, bodyguards, agents and ranch hands who will do whatever it takes to see justice served."

"Whoa, back up a step there. Covert Cowboys, Inc.?" Big Tex slapped his hat against his thigh. "Sounds kind of corny to me. What's the punch line?"

"No punch line." Hank stood taller, his broad shoulders filling the room, the steel in his eyes indisputable. The man was on the up-and-up. "Let's just say that I'm tired of justice being swept under the rug."

Ben shook his head. "I'm not into vigilante justice, or circumventing the law."

"I'm not asking you to. The purpose of Covert Cowboys, Inc. is to provide covert protection and investigation services where hired guns and the law aren't enough." Hank's gaze swept over each of the men in the room. "I handpicked each of you because you are all highly skilled soldiers, cops and agents who know how to work hard, fire a gun and are familiar with living on the edge of danger. But mostly because of your high moral standards. You know right from wrong and aren't afraid to right the wrongs. My plan is to inject you into situations where your own lives could be on the line to protect, rescue or ferret out the truth."

Ben stood, his body tense, his first reaction to the older man's words to leave and never look back. "I'm not a vigilante, despite what the news says."

"I'm not hiring you to be one," Hank said. "I'm asking you to join CCI as a protector, a man willing to fight for truth."

"Truth, huh?" Zach said. "It's hard to find people who care about truth anymore."

Hank's lips thinned. "My point, exactly."

"Tell me, why should I work for you?" Ben asked.

The older man's shoulders straightened and he looked directly into Ben's eyes. "I care about truth and justice." He walked to the desk in the corner and lifted four folders. The first he held out to Ben. "Are you in?"

What did he have to lose? Ben had nothing to go back to in Austin. No job, no family. Nothing. Against his better judgment, Ben nodded. "I'm in."

Hank handed him the folder. "Your first assignment is on the other side of the county working undercover on the Flying K Ranch. As far as everyone else knows, you're hiring on as a ranch hand. Your job is to help get the ranch operational, but most of all to protect the woman who just inherited it."

"Sounds easy enough."

"Don't count on it. This county is in need of cleanup. I'm hoping you gentlemen will be the men to help in that effort. It's our first challenge for CCI." Hank stared at the other men. "Who else chooses to take on the challenge?"

One by one the men threw their hats in the ring and grabbed a folder.

Ben opened the file and stared down at the image of a beautiful woman with long strawberry-blond hair, green eyes and skin as pale and smooth as porcelain. His gut told him he was stepping into waters way over his head. What did he know about providing protection to a woman? He'd been a street cop, not a bodyguard. Hell, he hadn't been able to protect his own family. A knot of regret twisted in him, but he asked, "When do I start?"

"Tonight. Grab your gear and get on over there, she should have arrived today."

Ben's eyes narrowed. "You were sure I'd take the job?"

"If not you, I'd be out there doing it myself. Don't get me wrong. I won't ask any of you to do anything I wouldn't be willing to do myself."

Ben clapped his hat on his head and headed for the door. It was a job. He didn't have to like it; he just had to do it until he found something else.

"'The cow dog saved the little girl and became her very best friend. The end.'" Kate Langsdon closed the book and set it on Lily's nightstand. "Now it's time for little girls to go to sleep." She leaned over and kissed her daughter's forehead, her heart squeezing in her chest with the amount of love she felt for this pint-size person with the long, loose curls of silky, strawberry-blond hair, much like her own.

"Mommy?" Lily yawned and rubbed her emerald-green eyes. "Can I have a cow dog?"

"Sure, sweetie. Just as soon as we can find one as good as Jess the cow dog." Kate switched the light off on the nightstand and straightened her aching back, got up and headed into the bathroom. The past few days had been strenuous and emotionally draining, the amount of work taking the spunk right out of her. She'd driven from Houston to Wild

Oak Canyon, Texas, cleaned a house that had been standing empty for two months, emptied as much as she could of the moving van she'd rented and poked through the belongings of a man she'd never known and never would.

Her father.

Tears welled in Kate's eyes. For years, she'd thought her father dead. All this time, the man had been living in South Texas on a ranch near Big Bend National Park.

Kate dug her hand in her pocket and thumbed the key she'd received a week ago in an envelope from an attorney, including a letter, last will and testament and one corrupt video disk. The day that package arrived everything in Kate's life had changed.

She pulled the key from her pocket and tossed it into her makeup kit, stripped out of her dirty jeans and climbed into the shower. She stood for a long time as the warm spray washed down over her body, releasing the stiffness from her shoulders and tempering the ache in her lower back.

She wished all her worries could wash away with the water. As she stood in her father's house, on the ranch he'd bequeathed to her, she wondered if she'd done the right thing bringing Lily here.

She'd come to start over and to find answers. For one, what did the key fit? The video had been all static and with a brief glimpse of her father, but it cut off before her father could tell her what the key belonged to. Her father's letter left instructions for her to get help from the only man he trusted, Hank Derringer, the owner of the Raging Bull Ranch in Wild Oak Canyon. He'd help her with whatever she needed.

She hadn't called Mr. Derringer at first, taking a day to digest the fact that her father hadn't died when her mother had told her. The news had been so shocking that it took that long for it to sink in. Contacting his trusted friend was the furthest thing from her mind.

Until someone broke into her apartment in Houston while she had been at work and Lily had been at day care.

When she'd come home to find the apartment she and Lily had called home for four years looking as if the place had been tossed in a Texas-size salad bowl, she'd been angry and scared.

How dare someone break into her home? Kate knew she couldn't stay in the apartment, not after it had been violated and especially not knowing the reason. Nothing had been taken, as far as she could tell.

She'd packed up her daughter, boxed their belongings and headed west to Wild Oak Canyon and the Flying K Ranch to find the answers. How permanent this move proved to be was up to what she found, but she'd quit her job and given up her lease before she left. Either way, she couldn't go back and pick up where she'd left off.

Alone in the world except for Lily, Kate had turned to the phone number of the stranger her father had recommended.

Hank Derringer had answered on the first ring. He'd tried to talk her out of coming to Wild Oak Canyon. When she'd insisted, he'd promised to send a cowboy to her, one who could help her get the ranch back up and running and provide the protection she and Lily needed. Her cowboy would be there before they turned in for the night. Or so Hank had promised. Kate wondered what kind of protection she needed on a ranch out in the middle of nowhere.

She'd waited as long as she could to take her shower and still the cowboy hadn't arrived and probably wouldn't until morning.

When the water grew tepid, Kate turned it off and grabbed for the fluffy white towel she'd unearthed from one of the boxes she'd brought with her in the moving van. Bent over, her head upside down to wrap her long hair in the towel, her hands froze. Was that a sound downstairs?

She strained to listen.

Nothing.

Kate shrugged, worried her imagination was getting the better of her. She continued towel drying her hair when something crashed below and a low curse followed.

Her breath caught on a gasp and her pulse raced. She'd turned out the lights on the main floor and locked all the doors before she and Lily had come up for the night. Whoever was down there was moving around in the dark. *Inside* the house.

Kate wrapped the towel around her and ran into the master bedroom she'd planned to share with Lily the first night until she could prepare another room just for her daughter.

Lily lay sound asleep, oblivious to the danger, the only light in the room the glow from the open bathroom door.

With nowhere to run, Kate quietly gathered her daughter, blankets and all, and hurried to the closet where she'd hung all of the clothing she'd brought with her next to those of her father's. Kate thanked her lucky stars that Lily slept soundly. The little girl didn't stir as Kate laid her down in the back corner of the closet, tucking the blankets around her, blocking her from view.

Once she had her daughter hidden, Kate tiptoed back to the nightstand, slid the drawer open and removed the 9 mm Glock she'd brought with her.

A board creaked on the stairs, sending Kate scurrying toward the door where she eased it closed.

Her hands shook as she alternated between holding up her towel and balancing the pistol. She wished she'd had time to dress, wishing more that she'd loaded the weapon. She prayed that the sight of it would scare a trespasser into leaving without hurting her or Lily. On second thought, she turned the gun around and held it by the barrel. Hitting the man would be better than pointing an unloaded pistol.

The doors down the hallway opened one by one. Kate held her breath as the intruder made his way toward the room she and Lily occupied. What she wouldn't give for cell phone reception.

Though, what good would it do when the sheriff wouldn't reach her ranch for fifteen to twenty minutes? She was on her own.

Where was the cowboy? Why hadn't he arrived already? Was the man moving down the hallway her cowboy? If he was, he had a lot of nerve barging in and sneaking around. He deserved the same as any thief and Kate would give it to him.

With Lily in the closet and her own hands shaking, Kate couldn't chance it. She had to divert attention and get the attacker away from the room where her daughter lay sleeping.

Kate prayed the man would give up and go away.

As she watched in horror, the doorknob turned. She wished it had a lock on it she could twist to buy her a little more time. Maybe not having a lock would work out for the better. She raised her arms and waited, her breath caught and held.

A dark figure stepped through the door. The man wore a ski mask. Anyone in a ski mask meant trouble.

As soon as his head cleared the entrance, Kate slammed the butt of the pistol down on his skull so hard the gun bounced out of her hands and skittered across the floor.

The man lurched forward and dropped to his knees.

Kate flung the door wide and leaped past the intruder.

Before she could take two steps, a large hand snagged her ankle.

Her forward momentum brought her down hard, knocking the breath from her lungs. She clawed at the carpet, kicking with all her might with her free foot, landing a couple hard heels in the attacker's face.

His grip loosened and Kate scrambled to her feet, running as fast as she could for the stairs, thankful and terrified when she heard the intruder's footsteps behind her.

She had to get the man as far away from Lily as possible.

If he hurt Kate, maybe he'd leave her for dead and never find the little girl hiding in the closet.

Kate took the stairs two at a time, missing the last one, toppling to the floor and wasting precious seconds.

The man above her came crashing down the steps and leaped over the railing to land beside her.

Kate swallowed her scream, fearing she'd wake Lily. She rolled to the side, her fingers wrapping around the cord of a lamp.

She yanked the lamp toward her, grabbed the base and turned in time to see the man flying at her. He landed on top of her, knocking the wind from her.

With her hand still around the base of the lamp, Kate swung as hard as she could. The ceramic lamp made contact with the ski mask and bounced off, crashing to the wooden floor, shattering into a million fragments.

Out of options, Kate remembered the self-defense training she'd taken when Lily was little. She knew she was the only one there to defend her small daughter. With the desperation of a trapped mother bear, she freed one hand and jabbed her thumb into the man's eye.

He yelled and punched her face.

Pain radiated across her cheekbone, her vision blurred and Kate knew she wasn't going to last much longer. For Lily, she tried to hang in there, forcing the darkness back, struggling beneath the weight of her attacker.

As the intruder reeled back to hit her again, Kate squeezed shut her eyes.

Before the fist connected with her face, all the weight on top of her shifted backward.

Kate's eyes popped open.

The man in the ski mask fought against another man wearing a black T-shirt and a cowboy hat. Fists flew, and bodies banged against the old furniture. The cowboy hat flew across the room, landing in a corner.

Kate sucked in air, filling her lungs and clearing her fuzzy thoughts. She scrambled to her feet, clutching the towel around her, searching for a weapon of any kind. Her hands wrapped around the legs of an end table. She lifted it high and waited for the right moment.

The two men tumbled and flew around the room, knocking over furniture. With the lights out, Kate could barely tell who was who.

Then her rescuer hit the floor on his back and the man in the ski mask pulled a knife from his belt, the metal glinting in a ray of moonlight shining through a gap in the curtained window.

Kate's heart thudded against her rib cage.

The man in the ski mask closed in on Kate's rescuer.

Without thinking past saving the man on the ground, Kate rushed for the one with the blade and slammed the end table down over his head with enough force to break the small table into several pieces.

The attacker dropped to his hands and knees. He swung his arm out, clipping Kate in the back of her legs.

She fell hard, her head hitting the corner of a coffee table. As she landed, she heard shuffling of feet and tried to rise to see what was going on. When she lifted her head, her vision swam.

No. She couldn't give up now.

Pain radiated from the back of her head. She closed her eyes, praying for them to clear and let her get back into the fight. Lily depended on her.

Hands gripped her arms. Kate struggled, but the grasp was strong. Too strong for her to fight off.

"Shh. It's okay. I'm not going to hurt you." The voice was a deep rumble, the tone rich and warm, resonating from deep in his chest, wrapping her in a reassuring blanket.

"Bad guy?" she asked, without opening her eyes.

"He's gone." A hand brushed a wisp of hair out of her

eyes. "Are you okay?" The same hand trailed softly over her cheekbone where the masked man had punched her.

Kate winced, and she opened her eyes to stare into the bluest eyes she'd ever seen. Her breath caught in her throat, and not out of fear. "Who are you?"

"Ben Harding. Hank Derringer thought you could use my help."

Thank God. The cavalry had arrived.

Chapter Two

Ben stared down at the woman, her long wavy strawberry-blond hair lying in damp ringlets against the wood floor. Wrapped only in a fluffy white towel, she looked like a fallen angel, her creamy smooth skin begging to be touched, the towel riding up her shapely thighs.

"You're staring." The woman blinked up at him, her fingers pulling the edges of the towel together over her chest. She tried to sit up, pressed a hand to the back of her head and sank back. "Must have hit harder than I thought."

"I'll call for an ambulance."

She shook her head and winced. "No. I'll be all right, just give me a minute." One arm rose to cover her eyes. The top edge of the towel slipped lower over the swell of her breasts, capturing Ben's attention.

He really needed to focus on the situation, not the female lying almost naked at his feet, which proved hard when the woman had a great figure and very touchable skin. A pang of guilt and sadness knotted his gut. He hadn't felt like touching a woman in more than two years. Not since… "Any idea what the guy was after?"

"None," she answered, the arm dropping to her side. "I'm just glad he's gone and you're here. I'm Kate Langsdon." She held out a hand, a frown denting her pretty brow. "What took you so long?"

"I just got the assignment an hour ago."

"Well, Mr. Harding, I'm glad you came when you did. Any later and…" She shrugged and tried to sit up again. "I have to get up."

"You should stay put and let me call an ambulance."

"No, I have to get upstairs."

"Why the rush?"

"I just need to." She sat up, swayed and started to fall back. "Damn it, I can't be dizzy."

"Pigheaded woman." Ben caught her before her head hit the floor.

"Stubborn man," she whispered.

He scooped her into his arms and lifted her off the floor.

She tensed, her arm automatically circling his shoulder. "You don't have to carry me. I'm perfectly capable of standing on my own two feet."

"Not with a knot on your head and a crazy determination to get upstairs."

"Give me a minute and I'll argue this point." Her uninjured cheek lying against his chest belied her ability to put up much of a resistance. Her free hand struggled to keep the towel in place.

Ben ignored her protest and carried her up the stairs. "Which room?"

She sighed. "Last one on the landing. And really, I can get there on my own."

"No need. From what Hank told me, I'm the hired hand, here to help rebuild a ranch and protect its owner."

"Hank's words?"

"Right." His lips twisted, a frown creasing his forehead. "Let me do my job."

She chuckled, a smile curling her lips, making her face shine even with the nasty bruise turning her cheek purple. "Somehow, I don't think carrying a woman to her bedroom is part of the job description." The smile faded. "But thanks."

For a brief moment the sun had shone in the woman's face, tugging at a place Ben thought buried for good with his wife and daughter. He shook the thought from his head and turned left on the landing.

When they crossed the threshold into the room, the woman twisted in his arms, her gaze darting toward the closet.

The door was open, blankets spilled from inside, some half-dragged out on the floor. "Let me down." She pushed against his arm, her nails digging into his skin.

"I will, but I'm not dropping you."

"Let me down." She shoved harder.

He lowered her feet to the floor, his arm remaining around her waist.

She stood for a moment, swaying, and then lunged for the closet, her eyes wide, her face tense. "Lily?" Her voice was strained, desperate.

"Who's Lily?" he asked.

Kate didn't answer as she dove into the back of the closet, rifling through blankets. When her face appeared at the edge of the closet door, it was pale and pinched. "Lily?" She leaped to her feet and nearly fell on her face.

Ben was there to catch her, his arms crushing her against his chest. "Who's Lily?"

"Mommy?" A tiny voice called out from the bathroom. "Mommy?"

Kate's head came up and she fought her way out of Ben's arms, dropping to her knees in front of a little girl with a mass of golden-red curls very much like her mother's drying wispy locks. She stood silhouetted against the light streaming from the bathroom, like an angel descended from heaven.

"Oh, Lily." Kate hugged the child to her.

Sweet Jesus. Hank hadn't said anything about a little girl. Ben stood like stone, his feet rooted to the floor, unable to move, forgetting how to breathe.

The little girl was about the age of Sarah before she'd been murdered. Though his Sarah was as different from Lily as night and day, they were about the same size and age.

Before Sarah had been killed. She'd been four years old. She would have been six now, if a man Ben had captured and had subsequently been released on a technicality hadn't targeted Ben and his family.

Ben hadn't been home when his wife and daughter had been brutally stabbed to death. Had he been, he'd have killed the murderer with his bare hands, just like he'd killed the man who'd murdered fifteen-year-old Angelica Garza.

Seeing Kate Langsdon on the floor holding the little girl in her arms brought back too many painful memories. Ben's feet moved one at a time as he backed toward the door. With his heart lodged in his throat, he couldn't breathe or think. His gut told him to run as far from Kate and Lily Langsdon as he could get.

Before he reached the door, the curly-haired angel noticed him for the first time. "Mommy, who's that man?"

Kate eased her hold on her daughter and looked up at Ben, the fear of a few moments ago still evident in her pale face. "That's Mr. Harding. He's the man who came to help us on the ranch."

"Are you going to help my mommy?" she asked, her gaze open, direct, piercing the wall wrapped tightly around Ben's heart.

He yearned to run and keep running until the child's trusting eyes were erased from his mind. But he knew he couldn't leave this little girl and her mother when the intruder he'd chased off earlier might return.

"Yes, ma'am. I'm here to help your mommy." He nearly choked on *mommy*. His daughter had called his wife Mommy. His daughter had looked at him with complete trust, as if he could never let her down.

But he had. He hadn't been there when she'd needed him most. He had been all about the job, bringing in the bad guys.

He'd never taken into account that the ones that got off might come back to haunt him. Until it was too late.

Kate's eyes narrowed. "Are you okay?"

No. Ben's gaze went from Lily to Kate. For a tough cop, used to facing down danger on the streets of Austin, he was more terrified of these two women than any criminal he'd ever confronted. "I'm fine." He cleared his throat. "I'll just bed down in the barn."

"No." Kate stood and swayed, her hand on her daughter's shoulder.

Before he could think through his actions, Ben was there, steadying her with a hand under her elbow, the other around her waist.

"Stay here. In the house." She leaned into him for a moment. When she'd steadied, she pulled away and looked up into his face. "Please."

Her green eyes pleaded with him, her hand on his arm burning a path through his defenses. How he wanted to leave, but couldn't. Despite his vow to never care again, he'd proved over and over he just couldn't honor that vow after all. Killing the high-powered child murderer was evidence. Damn Kate and Lily for making him care. "I'll stay on two conditions."

Her shoulders straightened. "Anything."

He scooped up the gun she'd dropped earlier and handed it to her. "First, put this away, take it to a pawnshop or learn to use it."

She took the gun from him, keeping her body between the gun and her daughter's curious eyes. "Check. I'll learn to use it." Her chin tipped upward. "And the second one?"

His gaze swept over her, taking in the smooth lines of her shoulders, the gentle swell of her breasts and the curve of her thighs peeking out from under the terry cloth. If he had any hope of staying neutral in this situation, he had to put distance between himself and Kate. She was too damned attractive.

He forced an uninterested rise of his brows. "If I'm going to get any work done around here, you have to keep your clothes on around me."

Kate gasped, hugging the towel closer, her cheeks flaming red.

"I'll be on the couch downstairs." He stepped out into the hallway and closed the door between them with a firm click.

Kate stared at the barrier between them for a long moment, stunned at the cowboy's abrupt words and departure. "As if I planned to be standing in front of him in nothing but a towel," she mumbled.

"Mommy, why was I in the closet?" Lily's hand slipped into hers and tugged, dragging Kate's mind back to what was important. Her daughter.

She scrambled for an answer that wouldn't scare her small daughter. "I thought it might be fun to pretend to be camped in a cave in the mountains."

Lily tipped her head to the side as if debating whether or not she believed Kate's lie. Then she smiled and pulled Kate toward the closet. "Will you camp in the cave with me, Mommy?"

"Oh, baby, I don't think so. I'm pretty tired and bed sounds more comfortable. You can sleep in the closet, if you want."

Lily stared from the bed to the closet and yawned, her eyelids sagging. "No, I'm tired, too. Maybe tomorrow."

Kate grabbed the blankets from the floor and flung them across the bed as best she could, tucking Lily in on the side away from the door.

As she pulled out a pair of pajamas that would fully cover her body, she thought of Ben Harding's condition. A spark of defiance shot through her and she replaced the pajamas in the drawer, reaching for the filmy light blue baby-doll nightgown she'd bought one hot, impulsive day in Houston.

She slipped the silky garment over her head, letting the towel drop to the floor, and recalled the feeling of being held in Ben's strong arms as he effortlessly carried her up the stairs to her bedroom. Her skin sizzled where his hands had been beneath her thighs and very nearly touching the side of her breast.

Now that she had time to think beyond defending her life, she realized the cowboy Hank had sent was everything a girl could dream of—tall, dark and handsome. Add a brooding, mysterious look in his blue eyes and he was devastatingly appealing.

She hadn't felt like this since…before her husband, Troy, had been killed in Afghanistan, a month before she'd delivered Lily. Four years ago. A wave of guilt washed over her for thinking such thoughts about a man who wasn't her husband. But, then, Troy had been dead a long time, she hadn't. The man downstairs had triggered a strong physical response she thought she'd never feel again.

Kate sucked in a deep breath and let it out, the tips of her nipples tight little points poking at the sheer fabric of the nightgown. She reached for the hem, telling herself that wearing the gown was asking for trouble.

Her hands stopped before they could lift it over her head. Who was she kidding? The man wasn't interested in her any more than she should be interested in him. He was there as the hired help. Hank had promised protection for her and Lily until they could figure out who was responsible for the break-in in Houston and now at the Flying K Ranch.

As she lay down on the sheets, her thoughts drifted to the man sleeping on the couch downstairs. He'd had a strange look in his eyes when he'd seen Lily. His brows had furrowed into a fierce frown, scary in its intensity. It hadn't looked like an angry frown so much as one of great pain and sorrow. What would cause such a look on a man's face?

She didn't know. In fact, Kate didn't know much of anything about her hired gun. Hell, she didn't know anything about Hank Derringer for that matter. This area was rumored to have a big drug cartel influence. Had she asked for help from one of the local mafia?

Kate lay staring at the ceiling, wondering what she'd done by bringing Lily here. Not that she'd been any safer in Houston. Not after her apartment had been ransacked.

A yawn nearly dislocated her jaw, forcing Kate to give up trying to make sense of all that had happened. Tomorrow she'd ask the questions burning in her mind. Who the hell was Ben Harding and what kind of hired hands did Hank Derringer provide? Even more importantly, did he have any hired hands that were a little older and less attractive?

Kate rolled over and punched her pillow before settling down. Her bruised cheek reminded her of the intruder and her near miss with death. She reached out and looped her arm over her daughter, pulling her close. If anything happened to Lily, she'd never forgive herself.

Tomorrow she'd start her search for answers.

Chapter Three

A knock on the door brought Ben off the couch and up on his bare feet in seconds. He must have fallen asleep after tossing and turning on the narrow couch. Every noise had kept him awake until way into the wee hours.

The sun shone through the filmy curtains, lighting his path through the boxes and furniture. From what he could see of the front porch, two men stood there in tan uniforms.

The local law enforcement.

As he pulled the door half-open, footsteps sounded on the stairs behind him.

"Who is it?" Kate descended the flight of stairs in a light blue baby-doll nightgown, pulling a robe over her shoulders that only came down to midthigh. Her creamy legs and the glimpse of her breasts through the thin material of the gown had Ben's jeans tightening.

With the door gaping, he had no choice but to open it the rest of the way.

The two men in tan uniforms stared at him, then their eyes drifted to the woman on the stairs behind him.

A flash of anger burned through his bloodstream and Ben moved to block their view as much as he could. "Can I help you?"

The bigger man stepped forward. "I'm Sheriff Fulmer, this

is Deputy Schillinger. We're here to see Katherine Langsdon."

Ben's eyes narrowed. "For what reason?"

The sheriff's lips pulled up on one side in a sneer. "Now, I guess that's between me and the lady."

"It's okay, Ben." Kate laid a hand on Ben's arm and stepped up beside him. "I wanted to call on them this morning anyway. We had a break-in last night."

"Sorry to hear that. Can you describe the perp?"

She shook her head. "No, he was wearing all black and a black ski mask."

"Not much I can do to help without a detailed description."

She tipped her head to the side. "Then why did you come out?"

"Ms. Langsdon, as the only living relative of the late Kyle Kendrick, you have been served." The sheriff handed her a thick envelope, his face poker-straight.

"What?" She took the packet, her cheeks blanching, making the bruise stand out even more.

"What's this all about?" Ben slipped an arm around Kate as she opened the envelope, every protective instinct on alert in the face of the sheriff and his deputy.

"Back taxes? The will said nothing about back taxes." She looked up at the sheriff.

"Sorry, Ms. Langsdon, I only deliver the bad news, I don't create it. Your father was the one who didn't pay. Since he left the ranch to you, you're responsible now."

Ben didn't like the sheriff's tone or the way the man hit her with the notice so soon after coming to her father's ranch.

"Twenty-seven thousand?" She snorted softly. "I can't afford twenty-seven *hundred*." Kate stared at the paper in her hands. "That would completely wipe me out and then some."

The sheriff shrugged. "You might consider selling this dump. Pretty young woman like you will find it difficult to manage a place this size all alone."

It was all Ben could do to keep from punching the sheriff for his patronizing words. Ben barely knew Kate, but any woman would resent the sheriff's inference that a woman couldn't run a ranch.

"I'm not alone." Kate clutched the envelope to her chest, her chin rising. "I have Ben." She edged nearer to Ben.

His chest swelled, his arm automatically tightening around her middle, pulling her closer to him.

The sheriff's brows rose. "Hired hands don't always stick around."

"He's not the hired hand. He's…" Kate's hand waved, in search of the right word.

Afraid she'd say he was her bodyguard, Ben finished for her, "I'm her fiancé. We will be working the ranch together."

The sheriff's eyes narrowed. "What did you say your last name was?"

Ben's lips twisted. "I didn't. Now, if you'll excuse us." He moved to shut the door.

The sheriff shoved his foot in the way. "Don't cross me, cowboy."

Ben's brows rose and he stared down at the boot in the doorway. "Did you have more business to discuss?"

The sheriff stared at Ben for a long moment, then replied, "No."

"Then have a nice day." Ben glanced down at the boot and back up at the sheriff. Ben's free hand clenched into a fist, ready to take on the arrogant sheriff if the need arose. He'd seen law enforcement officers who let the power of their position go to their heads. This sheriff appeared to be one of them. He made a mental note to watch the man. He could cause trouble for himself and for Kate.

The sheriff finally moved his foot. "I'll be seeing you around Wild Oak Canyon."

Ben shut the door, muttering, "Not if I can help it."

Kate turned away, her gaze on the legal document the

sheriff had given her. "Twenty-seven thousand dollars." She looked up at Ben, her eyes glazed. "That's more than I have in every savings account."

"Surely you have a thirty-day notice on it."

"Thirty days until they seize the property for back taxes owed." She shook her head. "I don't believe this. I should never have come."

"Can't you go back where you came from?" As he made the suggestion, his gut clenched. If Kate left, he wouldn't have to be around her. He could forget the way she made his body hum to life.

Kate shook her head. "No. I quit my job. They've already leased the apartment we lived in. Not that I'd go back. It's no safer in Houston than here."

"What do you mean?"

"I left Houston after my apartment was broken into and ransacked."

"In Houston?"

"Last week. The day after my father's will was read."

Ben didn't like it. Hell, she wasn't any safer in Houston than in Wild Oak Canyon. Ben resigned himself to being her protector until he could convince Hank he had the wrong man for the job. "Was your Houston apartment in a bad neighborhood?"

Kate shook her head. "I hadn't had any problems in the four years I lived there. Whoever did it tore everything apart."

"Any writing on the walls or threats?" Ben asked.

"No. They even ripped the cushions on my sofa. Every drawer was tossed, even the contents of the refrigerator."

"They're looking for something," Ben stated. "The day after your father's reading, you say? Did your father leave you anything besides this ranch?"

Kate's eyes widened. "Yes." Before Ben could question her, she ran up the stairs.

The blood racing through Ben's veins had nothing to do with whatever item she might have received from her father and more to do with the way her bottom swayed side to side and the vision of smooth, creamy skin visible along the curves of her legs. "More clothes. She damn well better wear more clothes," he muttered.

Kate paused at the top of the stairs, glancing down at Ben, her brows dipping. "Did you say something?"

"I'll get my clothes on." He strode back to the couch he'd spent the better part of the night lying awake on, thinking of the sexy legs on a woman he had no business looking at that way.

Hank Derringer was paying him to provide protection from a problem, not to become the problem or one more thing Kate had to be protected from.

He pulled his T-shirt on over his head, calling himself every kind of fool. If he had any cell phone reception at all, he'd be calling Hank and asking for a different assignment. One with a less attractive woman and…no kids.

"Hi."

Speak of the devil.

Ben's head poked through the neck of his T-shirt and he stared down at the pint-size version of Kate. Light reddish-blond curls lay in bright disarray around the child's shoulders.

She held out a brush. "Mommy told me to brush my hair."

Without thinking, Ben took the brush from the girl. He'd brushed Sarah's hair so many times he could have done it with his eyes closed. He knew just how to ease the tangles free without making her cry.

His throat closed as an image of his dark-haired daughter flashed into his memories. God, he missed her.

Lily looked up at him, her green eyes so like her mother's. "Please?" She turned her back to Ben and fluffed her mane of red-gold hair out behind her, waiting expectantly.

Just like Sarah had.

All of the air left Ben's lungs as if he'd been kicked hard in the gut. Yet his hand moved, reaching out to lift a lock of silky red-blond curls. He dropped to his haunches and ran the brush along the strand, picking out the knots with care.

He hadn't felt this emotionally wrung out since Sarah and Julia had died. But the more he brushed Lily's hair, the more his shoulders relaxed and the tightness in his chest loosened.

By the time he finished working the tangles out of the child's hair, he could swallow again. "All done," he said just like he had when he'd brushed Sarah's hair.

"Thank you." Lily turned and hugged him tight, her fresh, baby-shampoo scent filling Ben's senses.

Over the top of Lily's head he spied Kate standing on the bottom step, her eyes round. Was that a tear trickling down her cheek?

Kate ducked her head, a hand swiping at the moisture. Seeing Ben brushing Lily's hair had hit her like a Mack truck. Lily's father had died before she was born. Kate had been a single parent from day one. Seeing someone else, especially a man, brushing her daughter's hair sent a flood of longing through her, for Lily and herself.

Lily didn't know what it was to have a daddy. Just like Kate. Kate swallowed hard on the lump forming in her throat. "Lily, sweetie, go get dressed."

Her daughter's face lit. "Are we going outside to play?"

Kate smiled and patted her daughter's head. "You can play, but I have work to do outside."

"Yay!" Lily darted up the stairs, her bright curls bouncing as she went.

Kate descended from the last step and held out her hand. "My father left this key for me and a video disk."

She dropped the key and the disk into Ben's hand.

"What does the key go to?" Ben turned it over in his fingers.

"I don't know. I've tried to watch the disk, but I couldn't get it to work. The letter from the attorney had a note from my father to contact Hank Derringer for help."

"Maybe Hank can get someone to look at the disk and see if they can pull the information off."

Lily was down the stairs again, wearing shorts, cowboy boots and pulling a shirt over her head.

"Stop, young lady," Kate ordered, afraid her daughter would miss a step and tumble the rest of the way down the stairs. "You can't go out without me, and I'm not dressed."

"Please, Mommy." Lily looked up at Kate with a slight pout on her pretty pink lips.

"I'll take her," Ben offered. "We can discuss the key later." He handed it back to her, setting the disk on an end table.

Kate curled her fingers around the key. "I'll be ready in a minute. I need to finish unloading the rental van and get it back to town."

Ben smiled and raised his hands palms upward. "I'm here to help."

Kate's heart skipped several beats as the man's smile transformed his face from frowning, brooding darkness to sunshine. "You should smile more often," she said without thinking.

Immediately, his face changed back into the brooding cowboy, his forehead creasing. "I find little to smile about these days."

Kate wondered what made him so sullen and sad but didn't want to push the issue, not when he'd thrown up a no-trespassing sign in the way his body stiffened and he turned away. He took Lily's hand in his. "Ready?"

The two left through the front door.

Yes, sir, the cowboy had issues. Hell, didn't everyone?

Kate climbed the stairs, her footsteps slow at first and speeding up as she neared the top. For the first time in months, she wanted to get outside and enjoy the sunshine and fresh air. She refused to believe the hired hand had anything to do with her sudden surge of energy.

A pair of jeans, a snug-fitting ribbed T-shirt and tennis shoes completed her outfit. After she pulled her hair up into a ponytail and settled a baseball cap over her head, she hurried out to join Lily and Ben, her steps light, eager to finish unloading and settle into her new life.

Ben and Lily squatted beside the moving van, pointing at something on the ground.

"That's a scorpion, Lily," Ben was explaining. "Don't try to touch or pick one up, they have a really bad sting."

Lily hunched over, staring at the insect crawling across the ground. She looked up and spied Kate. "Mommy, come see the scorpion."

Kate smiled and squatted beside her. With the three of them all gathered in a circle so close, her stomach knotted. This must be what it would feel like to be a family unit. Mommy, daughter and…daddy. Troy would have been a good father to Lily. He'd been so excited about the arrival of his firstborn, only to be robbed of ever seeing her.

Lily was a beautiful baby and an even prettier little girl with a grown-up sense of responsibility and a child's joy of exploring.

"The day's not getting any longer. I guess we better get this van unloaded so that I can return it to the rental center in town." Kate stood, pulled the padlock key from her pocket and unlocked the back of the van.

For the next twenty minutes, Kate and Ben worked in silence, carrying boxes and furniture into the house. Lily helped a little, then lost interest and wandered around the yard, picking flowers and investigating her new home.

Kate kept a close eye on her. After last night's break-in, she wasn't feeling exactly trusting of her new environment.

Lily had strayed to the corner of the house when Kate

and Ben hauled out the sofa with the repaired cushions she'd brought with her from her apartment.

Getting the sofa through the door took them several tries, tipping it in multiple directions, before they finally shoved the item through. When the sofa cleared the door frame, Kate tripped over a throw rug and landed on her bottom, the edge of the sofa coming down hard on her ankle. "Ouch!"

"Are you all right in there?" Ben called out over the top of the sofa.

"Yes, just not very graceful." Kate stood and put pressure on her ankle and felt pain shooting up her leg. She swallowed a yelp and lifted her end again. There was no time for injuries. The van needed to be back before three o'clock or she'd have to pay for another day's rental.

Once they got the sofa settled into the living room, Kate headed toward the door, trying to hide her limp.

Ben shook his head and pointed to the sofa they'd just placed. "Sit."

"I'm fine, just a little sore. It'll work itself out." When she tried to walk past him, he grabbed her arms and made her stop.

"Let me see." His grip was firm but gentle and his tone the same.

The warmth of his hands on her arms sent shivers of awareness throughout her body. "Really, it's fine," she said, even as she let him maneuver her to sit on the arm of the couch.

Ben squatted, pulled the tennis shoe off her foot and removed her sock. "I had training as a first responder on the Austin police force. Let me be the judge."

Kate held her breath as he lifted her foot and turned it to inspect the ankle, his fingers slipping over her skin.

"See? Just bumped it. It'll be fine in a minute." She cursed inwardly at her breathlessness. A man's hands on her ankle shouldn't send her into a tailspin.

Ben Harding was a trained professional. Touching a woman's ankle meant nothing other than a concern for health and safety. Nothing more.

Then why was she having a hard time breathing, like a teenager on her first date? Kate bent to slip her foot back into her shoe, biting hard on her lip to keep from crying out at the pain. Her head came very close to Ben's. When she turned toward him she could feel the warmth of his breath fan across her cheek.

"You should put a little ice on that," he said, his tone as smooth as warm syrup sliding over her.

Ice was exactly what she needed. To chill her natural reaction to a handsome man paid to help and protect her, not touch, hold or kiss her.

Whoa, there, girl. Kate jumped up and moved away from Ben and his gentle fingers, warm breath and shoulders so broad they could turn a girl's head. "I should get back outside. No telling what Lily is up to."

Ben caught her arm as she passed him. "You felt it, too, didn't you?"

Kate fought the urge to lean into him and sniff the musky scent of male. Four years was a long time to go without a man. "I don't know what you're talking about."

Ben held her arm a moment longer, then let go. "You're right. We should check on Lily."

Kate hurried, no, ran for the open door, her heart racing, her breathing ragged. Just as she crossed the threshold into the open breezy, South Texas sunshine, a frightened scream made her racing heart stop.

"Lily!" Kate burst out onto the porch.

The sound of engines racing up the gravel driveway greeted her. A man wearing a do-rag over his head with a bandanna pulled up over his mouth and nose straddled a huge motorcycle in the middle of the yard, holding a doll by its hair. He laughed, the sound so evil it made Kate's skin crawl.

"That's Lily's doll." Kate flew off the porch and would have scratched the man's eyes out if an arm hadn't circled her waist and yanked her back.

"Go back to the house. Now," Ben said into her ear, his voice tight around the command.

"But Lily—"

"Go." He shoved her back behind him.

Kate hesitated.

The roar of engines rose to a crescendo. An army of bikes swarmed into the yard, stirring up dust where the grass had long since died.

Kate ran for the house. Before she could reach the porch, a motorcycle cut her off. There must have been twenty bikes racing around the yard in a tight circle, trapping Ben and Kate in the center. The dust rose in a cloud, choking visibility to everything beyond.

Beyond panic, long past frightened, Kate screamed into the smoke screen, "Where's my child?"

Chapter Four

Ben had left his Glock on top of the refrigerator inside the house while they'd been working to unload the trailer. Now he wished he had it. Two unarmed people against a biker gang weren't good odds in anyone's experience.

A rider broke the ring, circled the pair and then swerved toward Kate.

Fear for her spiked his adrenaline and he lunged toward the motorcyclist. Grabbing the closest handlebar, Ben twisted it hard toward the man astride. The sharp turn on the forward-moving bike caused the bike to flip over, rider and all.

Ben snagged Kate's hand and pulled her closer to him into the center of the circle.

The man he'd toppled pulled himself out of the dirt, his face bleeding from where he'd crashed into the gravel drive. He glared at Ben and Kate and roared, veins popping out on his forehead.

Kate shrank against Ben. "Oh, God."

They had nowhere to go; the ring of motorcycles tightened. The man with the doll eased toward them, dark eyes glaring through the slit between his do-rag and bandanna. "You need to leave, lady, before it's too late." He ripped the head off the doll and flung it at Kate's feet.

Kate reached for the doll, but Ben held her back. "When

I make my move…run toward the house," he said into her ear. Anger surged and Ben threw himself at the lead man, knocking him out of his seat.

Kate ran.

Ben got one good, hard punch at the man's face before two goons ditched their rides and jerked him off their leader. Caught between two beefy Hispanic men, Ben struggled, twisting and kicking, determined to keep their attention long enough for Kate to escape.

Ben jabbed an elbow into the gut of the guy on his right.

The man loosened his hold.

Ben ducked beneath his arm. No sooner had he shaken free from his captors' hold than he was slammed to the ground from behind, a bull of a man hitting him low and hard.

The wind knocked from his lungs, Ben lay facedown in the dirt, willing his body to move. A foot in the middle of his back kept him from doing anything, especially refilling his starving lungs.

Kate screamed.

A shot of determination rocketed through Ben. He rolled onto his back; at the same time he grabbed the man's leg who'd planted his heavy boot into his back. With a hard twist, he sent the thug flying backward, landing hard on his butt.

Two more men grabbed him, hauled him up and yanked his arms behind him, hard enough that spasms of pain ripped through his shoulders.

The leader lumbered to his feet and stalked toward Ben. He hit him with a hard-knuckled fist, square in the jaw. Ben's head jerked back, hazy gray fog encroaching on his vision. Another punch to his gut would have had him doubling over, if he didn't have two big guys holding him up.

Through the torture, his gaze panned the yard, searching for Kate and Lily.

The bikers had broken the circle and raced around the

yard, running over bushes, ramming into a rose trellis. One drove up onto the porch and ripped the porch swing from its hooks.

Another cut off Kate's attempt to get to the house.

Kate shot a glance over her shoulder and dodged to the left.

The biker sped past her and spun to renew his attack.

Ben planted his feet in the dirt and struggled, twisting and turning in an attempt to go to Kate's rescue, his mind conjuring his wife's last minutes on the earth, fighting to protect their daughter.

Then, he hadn't been there to help Julia. His job now was to protect Kate. If only he'd been more vigilant and not lulled into believing danger wouldn't strike during the day-light hours.

Hell, the fight wasn't over.

The gang leader swung again.

Ben jerked to the side hard enough that the guy on his left tripped. The leader's blow hit his own man in the cheek-bone. The man yelled and grabbed his face with both hands, letting go of Ben.

Using the weight of the other man's body, Ben rolled into him and sent him flying over his shoulder.

Kate ran toward the road.

The biker who'd missed her straightened his bike and hit the gas. The back tire spun, then gripped the ground and shot forward.

Ben came at him sideways, plowing into the biker.

The bike and rider rolled over to the side, the rider mov-ing sluggishly in the dirt.

One down, nineteen to go.

Kate ran on, but another bike raced after her.

Ben wouldn't catch up before the biker reached her.

A loud air horn broke through the roar of racing motor-cycle engines, followed by a cloud of dust storming toward them on the gravel drive leading to the highway. Another air horn burst and a truck swerved around Kate, aiming straight for the biker in pursuit of the fleeing woman.

A shotgun's nose poked out of the passenger window and blasted a hole in the ground in front of the bike tire. As a result, the biker spun so fast, the back wheel whirled all the way around and out from under the rider.

The gang members Ben had thrown off caught up to him and knocked him to the ground. He came up spitting dirt and ready to tear into them. He swung again and again, pummeling one man in the face. When that one went down, he kicked out and sent the other sprawling on his backside.

Another shot rang out, peppering bird shot at the gang members.

One man yelped and sent his bike skittering out of the shooter's range.

The leader of the gang yelled something and circled his hand in the air, then pointed to the road.

All of the bikers revved their engines and rode out, leaving a lung-choking cloud in their wake.

Their leader left the yard, shouting, *"Dejar o te vas a morir!"*

As the dust cleared, the driver and passenger of the truck dropped to the ground.

Ben laughed, the effort making his split lip and sore rib cage hurt. He leaned against the gnarled trunk of a live oak tree, his knuckles bleeding and every muscle in his body screaming.

The driver was an older Hispanic man with a decided limp. The passenger, the one holding the shotgun, was a woman who could only be described as grandmotherly. Thank the lord for help in all shapes and sizes.

Ben's next thought went to Kate and Lily.

Kate rounded the back of the pickup and ran back into the

yard, tears making muddy tracks down her cheeks. "Lily!" she cried out.

A whimper sounded from the tree branches over Ben's head.

Hidden between the leaves was a little girl with a curly halo of hair, clutching a ball of fur to her chest, tears slipping down her cheeks. "Mommy?"

"Lily?" Kate skidded to a halt beneath the tree. "Oh, baby. I'm so glad you're okay." Kate grabbed a branch and started up the tree.

Ben snagged her arm. "Let me."

"I can do this."

"It would be better if I could hand her down to someone she knows."

Kate backed away and let Ben take the lead.

He ducked beneath the low-hanging branches and climbed upward. "Hey, Lily. How'd you get all the way up here?"

She hiccuped, her bottom lip trembling as she clutched the fuzz ball to the curve of her neck. "I followed Jazzy."

"Is Jazzy one of your toys?" He spoke in calm, soothing tones, careful not to grimace when a shard of pain rippled across his hands or ribs.

Lily shook her head. "No, Jazzy's not a toy."

A soft mewling erupted from the fur ball and little paws reached out to latch onto Lily's shirt.

"Jazzy's a kitten." Lily's eyes rounded as she stared down into Ben's eyes. "Can I keep her?"

Ben chuckled, his body hurting with every breath. He wanted to crush the little girl and the kitten to his chest and hold them there for as long as he could. He couldn't tell if the pain he was feeling stemmed from sore ribs, bruises or heartbreak. "You'll have to ask your mommy."

"Will you ask her for me?"

"You bet." Ben settled on a thick branch and wrapped his

legs around it before he reached out. "Come on. I think your mother wants to fix you lunch or something."

"I'm scared." She glanced around at the ground below her. "Are the bad men gone?"

Rage burned in Ben's throat as hot as acid but he fought to keep it from his face and voice. "Yes, baby. They're gone." This child should not have been exposed to the violence of those men.

She leaned toward him and stopped, her arm around the kitten that clung to her, its blue eyes as big around as Lily's. "You're bleeding."

"It's okay. It doesn't hurt, just a little cut."

"I want my mommy," Lily whimpered.

"I'm going to hand you down to her. Come on. You're so brave to save that kitten. Now let me be brave and save you from falling out of the tree."

Lily smiled. "Silly, I'm not falling out of the tree."

"Your mother thinks you will." He winked. "But I know better. You're good at climbing trees, aren't you?"

She nodded, then let him grab her around the waist and lift her onto the branch he sat on. He hugged her to him, relief washing over him in such a rush that his eyes glazed over and he couldn't see.

"Give her to me, please," Kate cried.

Ben blinked several times before he loosened his hold on the little girl and handed her down into Kate's outstretched arms.

Kate gathered Lily into a hug so tight, Lily grunted. She sat on the ground in the dirt and hugged her some more, tears trickling from the corners of her eyes.

"I'm okay, Mommy." Lily patted Kate's face. "See?" Her empty hand pressed against Kate's face, urging her to look into her eyes. "I saved the kitten." Her smile broadened. "Can I keep her? Her name is Jazzy."

"Sure, honey. You can keep her." Kate dashed the tears

from her cheeks and hugged Lily again. Then she climbed to her feet, lifting Lily to perch on her hip. "Come on, let's clean up."

Ben slid out of the tree and dropped to the ground beside the two, his hand going around Kate's waist. "You two going to be all right?"

"I hope so." Kate's eyes widened. "You're bleeding."

Lily grinned at Ben. "Told you."

Kate cupped Ben's cheek. "Come in the house and let me take care of your cuts before they get infected."

The light touch sent fire through his veins. Ben pushed her hand aside. "I'm fine. I'll just stay out here and see what I can do to clean up the mess they made." Anything rather than being close to Kate. She brought out too many feelings in him, feelings he'd thought long dead, emotions that made a man vulnerable.

The woman holding the shotgun waved her hands at them. "You three go get cleaned up and let us take care of the mess. Eddy and I can set things to rights in no time. Can't we, Eddy?"

The short Hispanic man had wandered off, picking up broken bush branches. *"Sí, señora."*

Ben stepped between the woman and Kate. "Could we at least know the names of our rescuers?" He tried to smile, his lip hurting with the effort. "I'm Ben Harding, Kate's my...fiancée."

"Oh, goodness, yes." The woman shifted the shotgun into her other hand and gripped Ben's hand in a firm, capable grasp. "Margaret Henderson. But most folks 'round here call me Ma or Marge. This here's Eddy."

"Mrs. Henderson, Eddy, glad to meet you." Ben nodded at the gun. "Good shootin'."

"No boys in my family, so my daddy taught all his girls to squirrel hunt." She grinned. "And I make a mean squirrel soup."

"I'll bet you do." Ben let go of her hand. "Thank you for showing up when you did. I think they were about to get the best of us."

"I don't know. You were holdin' yer own pretty well."

Ben didn't want to argue with the woman. He'd gotten his butt whipped and Kate would be in a world of hurt had Margaret and Eddy not come along when they did. Guilt with a hint of heartrending regret tugged at his empty belly. What made Hank think a washed-up cop was the right man for this job? It had taken an old woman with a shotgun to chase off the latest threat. Some bodyguard he'd turned out to be.

Margaret smacked Ben on the back. "Twenty-to-one odds needs a little more encouragement than bare fists. Don't let it get ya down. Question is why they were here in the first place."

Eddy stuck a long blade of grass between his lips and rocked back on his heels. "Their leader shouted *'Dejar o te vas a morir'* as he left." The man had a decided Mexican accent.

Kate shook her head. "I don't know Spanish. What does it mean?"

Eddy's gaze captured Kate's, his lips tightening for a moment before he spoke. "Leave or you will die."

Kate's heart sank into her belly. Holy smokes, what the hell had she done to the bikers to warrant a death threat?

"Well, now, isn't that a nice way to welcome the new neighbors." Marge turned to face Kate, the stiff, tough persona fading with the softening of her eyes. "You must be Kate."

Kate held on to Lily, refusing to let her child out of her sight for even a moment. Her legs still shook and she couldn't keep her hand from trembling when she held it out to Margaret. "Should I know you?"

"Kate Kendrick—" the woman folded Kate's hand in both of hers "—you're the spittin' image of your father."

Kate shook her head. "I go by Kate Langsdon." She gripped the woman's hand with her free one. "Did you know my...Kyle Kendrick?" She still couldn't manage to refer to him as her father. Throughout her life, her mother had told her that her father had died in a car wreck. Growing up without a father hadn't given her any practice saying the word. And for the past four years, Lily had been without a father of her own.

"Know him? I worked for him until the day he was m—" The older woman's eyes widened and she clapped a hand over her mouth. "Sorry." Her glance moved to Lily, and her hand fell to her side. "I worked for Mr. Kendrick until he passed. He was a good man."

Kate bit her lip, wanting to refute Mrs. Henderson's statement. What man would willingly walk away from his daughter and never have contact with her? In Kate's mind, that didn't make a good man.

"Thank you for coming to our rescue." Kate smiled and turned to Ben. "Now, let's get you inside and doctored up."

The kitten Lily had been holding mewed.

An answering meow came from beneath the porch and a brightly colored calico cat stepped out of the shadows.

The kitten clawed at Lily.

"Ouch." Lily held the kitten away from her shirt.

Kate pointed to the cat. "That must be the kitten's mother."

Lily hugged the fur ball to her, her brows pulling together in a mutinous frown. "Jazzy is *my* kitty."

"Honey, you have to let her go to her mama."

"But I want a kitten."

"Jazzy will be your kitten, but you'll have to let her be with her mama until she gets bigger."

"I want her to come in the house and sleep in my bed."

"When she doesn't need her mother anymore. You can come and play with her outside until then."

The kitten dug her claws into Lily, scrambling to get to her mother.

"See, she misses her mother." Kate leaned Lily away from her. "How would you feel if someone wouldn't let you come to your mother?"

Lily stared at the kitten and the calico mother cat, meowing over and over. "I'd feel sad."

"And the kitten is sad because you won't let her go to her mother."

Lily wiggled in Kate's arms, so she set her daughter on the ground.

Plucking the kitten's claws from her shirt, Lily settled the animal on the ground.

As soon as she was loose, the kitten ran for her mother, curling in and around the cat's long, sleek legs.

"See how happy Jazzy is?" Kate knelt beside her daughter.

"Can I play with her after lunch?"

"You sure can." If the bikers weren't back or an intruder wasn't rummaging through the only home they had to go to. Kate's chest tightened. "We'll bring food out for Jazzy and her mother."

Lily slipped her hand into Ben's and one into her mother's. "I'm hungry. Can we eat now?"

Kate almost laughed at how quickly Lily forgot the bad men on motorcycles, all her concentration on eating and getting back outside to play with her kitten. How simple to be a child and forget about all the horrible things adults could do to each other.

Ben glanced over the top of Lily's head. "She'll be all right."

The biker's warning echoed in Kate's mind. "I hope so."

Chapter Five

Kate led the way into the ranch house. As soon as she passed through the door, Lily shook her hand free and ran to the bathroom. Kate and Ben followed, filling the tiny room.

Lily stood on a small plastic step, just the right height to boost her little body up to the sink. She pumped liquid soap onto her hands and turned on the faucet, splashing water over her arms and shirt. "Do kittens like milk?"

"I suppose they do," Kate replied, her voice soft, reassuring and less shaky than it had been in the yard after being terrorized by the biker gang.

Ben's gut clenched. He should have been ready—he could have handled the situation better. He reached out and grabbed her hand. "I'm sorry."

Kate's brows wrinkled. "For what?"

"Letting it go that far."

She dragged her hand out of his, closed the toilet lid and pointed at it. "Sit."

Obediently, he did, amazed at the strength in her tone.

While washing her hands, she chewed on her lip, tears welling in her eyes. She dashed them away, apparently not wanting him to see them. Tough tone and tears didn't add up. Ben's chest squeezed. This woman had been scared out of her mind, but she refused to show it.

Lily climbed into Ben's lap. "You have a boo-boo on your mouth." She poked a finger at the drying blood.

The child felt right, her legs dangling over his knee, her feet swinging in and out. As quickly as she'd come, Lily slid off his lap and left the bathroom.

"Stay in the house, Lily," Kate called out.

"I will. I'm going to my room to play with my dolls."

The sound of footsteps on the stairs echoed through the old house.

Kate snatched a clean hand towel from the shelf over Ben's head, leaning so close, the scent of herbal shampoo wafted over him.

Her breasts brushed against his shoulder and he gasped.

Kate jerked back, towel clutched in her fingers. "Did I hurt you?"

"No," he said through clenched teeth. The pain she'd caused had nothing to do with flesh wounds. She'd stirred his heart to life and that was more painful than a broken bone or knife stabbing. He'd thought his heart was firmly locked away after the deaths of his wife and daughter.

Now he sat at the tender mercy of a woman and her daughter, reminding him with every move, every touch and soft word of all he'd lost.

She dampened the towel in the water and touched the cloth to the corner of his lip, dabbing gently to remove the dried blood.

"Lily's a great kid," he said.

"I know." Kate's gaze focused on his wounds, one hand steadying herself on his shoulder. Warmth filtered through his chambray shirt to his skin. Ben's jeans tightened and his pulse quickened.

"Some bodyguard I am," he said.

When he glanced into her eyes, he caught her staring down at him.

"You were outnumbered. You couldn't fight them all."

"I should have had my gun on me at all times," he countered.

"And they might have used it on you or Lily."

"Or you."

"I'll make an ice pack for that jaw. Any other injuries?"

The longer she stood there close enough to touch, the harder it was not to reach out. "No." He shook his head and stood, wincing, his hand automatically rising to press against his ribs.

Kate's brow furrowed. "Liar. Let me see." She pushed his T-shirt up, tucking it beneath his arms.

A bruise the size of a grapefruit was making its dark purple appearance against his skin and everything beneath the mark ached.

"Damn, Ben, you could have a broken rib." She dipped the towel beneath the faucet again, wrung it out and pressed it to his side, her fingers sliding over the bruise. "Does that hurt?"

Ben grasped her fingers and held them away from his skin. "Yes," he lied. Her touch wasn't what hurt, it was the effect she was having on him. If he didn't get away soon, he'd be hard-pressed to walk away without kissing her.

"Let me take you to the clinic in town. They must have an X-ray machine." She tugged her hand free and pressed the cool towel to his side, all her focus on his injury.

Past his level of endurance, Ben tipped her chin up. "I don't need a doctor. I'm not going anywhere."

When her green-eyed gaze met his, he realized his mistake. Her lips parted, and what she might have said next faded away on a sigh.

Ben bent and brushed his lips across hers. He'd only wanted a taste. But like water to a desert flower, the more he tasted the more he wanted.

His fingers curled around the back of her neck, tugging at her hair, tipping her head back, giving him more access to her lips, her throat and the pulse beating wildly at the base.

She leaned into him. Her fingers pressed against his chest, the tips curling into his skin, not enough to hurt, but enough to ignite a flame he'd thought long burned out.

As fire spread through his veins, his arms tightened around her, his lips going from soft and gentle to crushingly hard, desperate to wipe out the stab of guilt that ravaged him from head to toe.

"I'm sorry, Julia," he said against her lips. "I'm so sorry."

The woman in his arms stiffened, her mouth moving away from his, her hands pressing against his skin.

"Let go of me," she said, her voice ragged, her tone strained.

Ben backed up, his hands dropping to his sides. "I'm sorry. That shouldn't have happened."

"Damn right, it shouldn't have." Kate's hand shook as she swiped the back of her hand over her bruised lips. "I don't know who Julia is, but I'm not her." She turned to walk out of the bathroom.

Ben caught her hand. "You're right. I had no business kissing you." Not when he still had feelings for his dead wife. Feelings that amplified his guilt for having kissed this stranger. "It won't happen again."

Without facing him, she jerked her hand free. "I don't think this arrangement will work after all."

"I understand. I'll talk with Hank about a replacement this afternoon."

"Please." Her shoulders rose and fell as if she sighed deeply, then she left the room.

Ben's fists balled. He wanted to hit something, but his knuckles were already like raw meat. He wasn't sure he could handle any more pain, both physical and emotional.

Too much about Kate and Lily reminded him of Julia and Sarah. The sooner he left the Flying K Ranch the better off they both would be.

Images of the intruder on the first night and the terror of

the motorcycle gang nagged his conscience. Would Kate's next hired gun take better care of her? Would he try to kiss her and forget why he'd come?

KATE RAN UP the stairs and peeked in at Lily. Her daughter sat at her little table with her miniature tea set laid out. A teddy bear and two dolls occupied the other seats.

Satisfied Lily was okay, Kate slipped past and into her own room, closing the door behind her. She leaned against the panel and pressed her fingers to her burning cheeks.

He'd kissed her. Her bodyguard had kissed her.

What had her running scared was that she'd liked it. So much so that she'd kissed him back, practically crawling up his body to get closer.

She covered her softly swollen lips and moaned.

It had been four years since she'd known the touch of another man's kiss, the feel of big, strong hands on her skin.

Her body burned with a need she thought had been buried with her husband. Kate squeezed her eyes shut and tried to picture Troy's face, a sob rising up her throat when the only face she envisioned was Ben's.

Kate opened her eyes, her gaze darting around the bedroom to the framed photograph of her and Troy on their last vacation together. They'd gone to the coast, playing in the sun and sand as if there'd be no tomorrow. Tomorrows for Troy had ended with an improvised explosive device that detonated beside his convoy. He'd been killed instantly. One week before he was due to come home. One month before his daughter's birth. Two days before their third anniversary.

Troy smiled back at her from the photograph, his light gray eyes and sandy-blond hair so different from the dark hair and stormy-blue eyes of the man downstairs.

Kate hugged the frame to her breast, again trying to recall Troy smiling down at her as he'd kissed her goodbye. Even holding Troy's photo, Kate couldn't see him. Her mind fixated on the dark-haired, brooding man who'd come to help her keep Lily safe in their new home.

Kate set the photo on her nightstand and hurried into the bathroom. She didn't have time to worry about why her memories of Troy were fading. She had a daughter to take care of, one who needed her to make lunch.

She stared into the mirror and almost cried of fright. Her face was smudged with dirt, her eyes red-rimmed and puffy from tears of joy at finding Lily safe in a tree.

Kate scrubbed her face with cool water, brushed her hair and secured it in a ponytail at her nape. Clean-faced and re-freshed, she took a deep breath and resolved to act as if nothing had happened. No more kisses would be exchanged and life would go on as usual.

When she passed Lily's room, her daughter no longer sat at her table, the tea set abandoned.

Her heartbeat quickening, Kate hurried down the stairs.

A quick perusal of the living room found it empty. Only Mrs. Henderson in the kitchen.

Fear pushed Kate out the front door.

Ben was hanging the porch swing that had been knocked down by the gang.

As soon as he settled the chain on the hooks, Lily climbed up on the swing and patted the seat beside her. "Will you swing with me?"

"I don't know." Ben glanced out at the dry Texas land-scape, only his profile visible from where Kate stood. The dark circles beneath his eyes and sad, faraway look tugged at Kate's heartstrings.

"Please?" Lily batted her eyes like a pro.

Ben chuckled and smiled. "When you put it like that… sure." He settled on the swing beside Lily and looped his arm over the child's shoulder, pulling her close.

A lump the size of a grapefruit lodged in Kate's throat and

she backed away, racing for the kitchen and a hand towel to dry quickly forming tears.

Marge stood at the kitchen counter, adding lettuce and tomatoes to thick slices of bread layered with lunch meat. "Ah, there you are. I hope you didn't mind me barging in and jumping right in. I worked here so many years, it feels more like home to me than my own house. I've missed coming out."

Kate's mouth watered. "Where did you get all that food?"

"I was the cook and I handled the grocery shopping for Mr. Kendrick. I figured with you just having moved in, you probably hadn't had time to visit the store to stock up. Eddy's a ranch hand. He wanted to check on the horses and cattle, so I asked him to bring me out after stopping for a few things at the market."

"A few?" Kate opened the pantry doors and checked in the refrigerator and gasped. "This isn't a few."

Mrs. Henderson blushed. "I'm sorry. It's kind of pushy of me, but I've been beside myself staying at home since Mr. K. passed. My husband retired last year and we just bump into each other too much. I *need* to work outside the home."

"I'm not sure I can pay you, and I don't expect you to work for free."

"Now, don't you worry none. Consider this a welcome home gift. And once Eddy gets the cattle rounded up and the fences mended, he'll give you a better idea of what this place can do to support you and your little one."

Tears filled Kate's eyes. "Why?"

"Like I said, Mr. Kendrick was a good man. Many times he'd spot me my mortgage payment when my man was out of work." The older woman sliced a sandwich in two and laid it on a freshly cleaned plate. "Now, you just sit right down there and have yourself a bite. You could stand to gain a pound or two." Marge patted her rounded figure. "Not that you want to put on as many as I have." She laughed and moved around the kitchen like one very familiar with its contents.

Ben entered, carrying Lily on his arm. "Someone is hungry. I wonder who it is."

Lily's hand shot up. "Me!"

He swung her up in the air and caught her.

Kate's heart warmed at her daughter's giggles. Oh, to be young enough to forget so easily. Today could have turned out very badly. Any one of them could have been hurt or killed. Thank God Lily had been climbing a tree, although Kate wasn't all that comfortable with a four-year-old climbing unattended. What if she'd fallen?

If the impact on the ground hadn't hurt her, the biker gang could have.

Ben set Lily on her feet and laid a hand on Kate's shoulder. "She's all right. I won't let anything bad happen to her."

"I know that." Kate's gaze followed Lily around the kitchen, but her mind was on the hand warming her shoulder. "I was just thinking that I should be mad at Lily for climbing a tree, but I can't find it in my heart to be. If she hadn't…" Kate glanced up into Ben's eyes.

A muscle in the side of his jaw twitched. "We'll have to do a better job of keeping an eye on her. She's a very active little girl. Aren't you, darlin'."

Marge trimmed the crust off a sandwich and cut it in triangles, then set it on a plate in front of Lily. "Eat up, half-pint."

"You'll spoil her," Kate protested.

"It's my biggest fault." Marge smoothed Lily's hair back from her forehead. "Never had any of my own. Guess I do go a bit overboard."

"It's hard not to, even when they're yours." Kate smiled at Lily. "She's all I've got."

Marge smiled. "You have Ben, too. When are the two of you lovebirds gonna tie the knot?"

Kate's face burned. She hated lying, but if it helped keep

the rest of the town off her back, she'd do it, and she didn't know Marge well enough yet to set her straight on the fake engagement. "We haven't set a date."

"No hurry, huh? Too many young couples meet each other one day, marry the next and file for a divorce within a year." Marge crossed her arms. "You're smart to wait. Seems Mr. Kendrick and your mama were in that category. Young and crazy stupid in love. Mr. Kendrick never considered whether his new bride would be happy out in the middle of nowhere Texas. She wasn't suited for the rugged life of a ranch owner. Too bad she didn't stay around long enough to find out."

"My mother never talked about my father. She told me he'd died in an automobile accident."

Marge shook her head. "Nearly broke Mr. K.'s heart when your mama left him. He didn't even know you existed until after your mother died and her lawyer notified him, or I'm sure he'd have done more to get to know you sooner."

"My mother's been dead for nearly five years. Why didn't he come find me then?"

Marge shrugged. "I asked him again and again. He just said the timing wasn't right. Might have been because he'd been doing a lot of traveling." The housekeeper leaned close. "He never said, but I think he worked for the government, secret service or something. He'd pack and leave a note that he'd be gone awhile. Never said how long, when he'd be back or where he was going."

"Any idea where he went?" Ben asked.

"I think he had business in Mexico. The man spoke Spanish like a native."

Kate frowned. How sad to learn about her estranged father from a stranger. Especially when he'd lived in Texas all her life and hadn't bothered to get to know his daughter even after he'd learned of her existence.

"Mrs. Henderson?" Ben began.

"Call me Marge. Please."

"Marge." Ben smiled. "What exactly happened to Mr. Kendrick?"

"Now, that's a very good question. You'll get a different answer depending on who you ask."

"What do you mean? Didn't a coroner determine cause of death?"

"The county coroner is a good friend of the sheriff. He'd put whatever the sheriff wanted him to put on the death certificate."

Kate's eyes widened. "I was under the impression Kyle Kendrick died of natural causes."

"The coroner stated he'd died of heart failure."

"And you don't believe him?"

"Oh, I'm sure Mr. Kendrick died of heart failure, but the cause of the heart failure, in my opinion, had nothing natural about it."

Ben pulled up a chair at the table and sat beside Kate. "Why do you say that?"

"The man had bruising around his throat. I'm sure his heart failed when his lungs could no longer get air."

Kate gasped, setting her sandwich on the plate, all hunger forgotten. "Someone choked him?"

"I watch enough crime scene investigation shows to know a man with bruises around his throat didn't run into a door."

"Did you say anything to the sheriff?"

Marge shook her head. "If they couldn't see what was in front of them, either they're just plain stupid or were in on the killin'. Sayin' somethin' to them wouldn't bring back Mr. K., and it might have bought me the same demise."

A chill slithered across Kate's skin. "Who would want to kill him?"

"I can't even imagine." Marge tidied the counter, talking as she went. "Mr. K. was quiet, but well-liked in the community by the few who got to know him. He never had a bad word to say about anybody. He was kinda reclusive, but that could be expected of a confirmed bachelor like himself." She paused and stared out the window. "Could be someone involved in the troubles around here."

Kate frowned. "Troubles?"

"The Flying K is smack-dab in the middle of an area known for drug trafficking from across the border." Mrs. Henderson glanced at Lily. "Maybe Mr. K. got cross-ways with one of them. They found him here in this house. No sign of forced entry, but the place was a shambles. It was like someone he knew killed him, then ransacked the house. As far as I could tell, the only thing missin' was the computer out of Mr. K.'s office. Eddy thinks it was Larry Sites, though why Larry would take the computer…" Mrs. H. shrugged. "The man could barely read, much less find his way around a keyboard."

"Larry Sites?" Kate shook her head, trying to take it all in.

"Larry was a ranch hand here at the Flying K. Worked with Eddy. But no one's seen him since the day we found Mr. K." Marge clucked her tongue. "Poor Mr. K."

A lead weight settled in Kate's belly. "The more I hear the more I'm beginning to think Lily and I need to move back to Houston."

"Oh, honey," Marge said as she laid a hand on Kate's shoulder. "I'd hate to see you go when you just got here."

"Mommy, can I go out now?" Lily asked, her hands and face covered in peanut butter and jelly.

"Sweetie, it'll have to be later. After you wash your hands and face, we're going to town. I have some business to do there."

Mrs. Henderson was there with a clean, wet washcloth before Lily could move a muscle, scrubbing the sticky jelly from her face and hands.

"What do you say to Mrs. Henderson?" Kate prompted.

"You missed a spot." Lily's tongue slid along her lips and she smacked them loudly.

Marge laughed and dabbed at the stickiness.

Lily jumped down from her chair and skipped toward the hallway. "Thank you for making lunch, Mrs. Henderson. It was delicious."

Kate pushed her plate away and stood. "Thank you for the sandwiches, Marge." She rummaged through drawers to find something to wrap hers in.

"Don't you worry about that. I'll put it away for later. You go on. The town rolls up its sidewalks at five o'clock. If you have business there, you need to skedaddle."

"We'll find dinner in town. No need to cook anything here."

"Will do, Kate." Marge gave her a hug. "I'm glad you're here. I've missed Mr. K. and you're the spittin' image of the man, only prettier."

Kate thanked her again and hurried out of the kitchen, her mind running through all Mrs. Henderson had said.

She should have looked this gift horse in the mouth before accepting it and moving out to Wild Oak Canyon in the middle of South Texas. Now that she was here, she had to make the best of it. First things first. She wanted to know more about her father's death and the people with whom he'd done business.

BEN FOLLOWED KATE out of the kitchen. "I have a bad feeling about this."

"You and me both." She stopped at the base of the steps. "I want to freshen up a bit, then I'll be down. I assume, as my bodyguard, you'll be coming with me to town?" This last question she spoke in a whisper.

"That's right."

"In my car or your truck?"

"My truck."

"Good. I'll meet you in five minutes." She ran up the stairs.

Ben almost groaned aloud at the sway of her hips. The woman was far too distracting for him to keep his mind on the task at hand. Julia hadn't been quite as curvy as Kate. Her frame had been slight, so much so that giving birth had been especially difficult. Their obstetrician recommended that she not have any more children due to her narrow frame and complications of high blood pressure and prenatal diabetes during pregnancy.

Ben had been disappointed, wanting a whole brood of children. But he'd hidden his regret well. The sight of baby Sarah, so perfect and pink, had been all he'd needed.

Until a brutal murderer had taken her away from him.

All these thoughts stemmed from the one short glimpse of Kate's swaying fanny.

He shook his head, squared his shoulders and climbed the stairs behind her, heading for the room she'd assigned to him where he changed into a clean shirt and jeans.

Once he'd smoothed his hair into a semblance of order, he stepped into the hallway and ran into Kate.

He knocked into her, throwing her off balance. Ben grabbed her and pulled her into his arms, crushing her against his chest, his heartbeat hammering through his veins. Had he hit her any harder, she would have fallen right over the railing and down to the hardwood flooring.

Once he had her securely in his arms, he couldn't make himself let go. Her curves fit him in all the right places, so soft and tempting.

She looked up, her lips inches from his. "What are you doing?" she whispered.

"Keeping you from falling over the rail." Ben couldn't believe how cracked his voice sounded. "I promise to be more careful in the future."

Her tongue swept across her bottom lip, moistening it. "Please."

"Please what?" Why hadn't he let go of her already?

"Be more careful." She dragged in a deep breath and stepped free of his arms, straightening her shoulders while tugging the hem of her blouse. "I need to get to town. I want to run by the bank before they close."

He nodded, his hands dropping to his sides, the heat still burning within. "I need to touch base with Hank while we're there."

"Good. Then let's get going."

At least one of them had the wherewithal to get past the awkwardness Ben had instigated.

"I'll get Lily." Kate dodged past him like a scalded cat and ducked into Lily's room.

"I'll be in the truck," Ben called out, taking the stairs two at a time. He breezed through the kitchen. "You need a ride back to town, Mrs. Henderson?"

"No. I see Eddy headed this way. I'm sure he'll be wanting to get home and he promised to take me. Don't worry none about locking up. I still have a key." She patted her pocket.

Ben almost frowned, but caught himself. "Are you the only one who has a key besides Ms. Langsdon?"

"As far as I know." Marge's brows furrowed. "Why?"

"Just wondered. I'll make a stop at the hardware store to buy all new locks and keys. Just for safe measure."

She nodded. "Don't want anything bad to happen to those girls."

Ben's jaw tightened. "No, we don't." Whether it was him or one of Hank's other cowboys taking care of her, it wouldn't hurt to change out the locks on the house.

He pulled his truck around the side of the house, got out and grabbed the booster seat from Kate's car, securing it in the backseat of his truck. He tucked his 9 mm pistol into the glove box.

Lily burst through the front door and skipped across the yard, all smiles, her light strawberry-blond curls bouncing around her shoulders. She wore a sundress with a bright yellow-and-white daisy pattern. She was all sunshine and happiness, oblivious to the dangers around her.

That's how a child should be—carefree and happy.

Ben's fingers tightened around the steering wheel, memories threatening to overwhelm him. Scenes in his mind he'd tried so hard to push away.

Kate followed Lily out the door. Her pretty red-blond hair was pulled up in a loose bun at the back of her head. She wore a pastel yellow sundress and sandals, looking like spring and everything right with the world.

God, he had to get Hank to find someone else to take this job. He wasn't cut out for this. It was too soon. Every time he looked at the mother and daughter, a knife twisted in his gut. Sadly, he feared it was already too late to walk away.

Ben couldn't imagine leaving them to whatever peril the wild Texas landscape, and even wilder men who'd already threatened her, had to offer.

He opened the back door, helped Lily up into the booster seat and buckled the belt across her lap.

"I'm impressed," Kate said as she inspected his work. "You did that like you've done it before."

Ben backed away and rounded the truck, wordlessly, his teeth clenched. He'd buckled Sarah in a hundred times, careful with his precious daughter, wanting to keep her safe in case of a traffic accident. Too bad he hadn't kept her safe from her killer.

Kate climbed up into the passenger seat, her brows puckered. "Did I say something wrong?"

"No." Ben sat behind the wheel, fighting for control. Finally, he shifted the truck into Drive.

Her brow remained puckered as she sat back.

Lily fell asleep in the backseat almost as soon as they hit the highway.

Ben's grip tightened on the wheel, his knuckles turning white. His gaze panned the long stretch of road, looking for any hidden hazards, man-made or in the terrain. As knotted up as he was, he'd exhaust himself before nightfall. He inhaled and let the breath out slowly, willing himself to relax.

When they neared the town of Wild Oak Canyon, he had his control back.

Until Kate spoke, her soft tones warming him inside and out. "I believe the bank is on the next corner."

Ben shook his head. "We're stopping at the sheriff's office first."

Chapter Six

Kate climbed down from the passenger seat before Ben could come around and open her door. He insisted on lifting Lily out of her booster seat. Still sleepy, the child stirred and lay across Ben's shoulder. Her eyelids fluttered, then closed.

The sight of Lily sleeping so peacefully on Ben's shoulder was sweet and disturbing. On the one hand the three of them gave the appearance of being a family. On the other, Ben wasn't a fixed variable in Lily's life. When they figured out what was going on and cleared the threat, Ben would be gone. Lily would wonder what she'd done to chase him off. She might even blame herself. Kate reached out. "I'll take her."

Ben turned away, refusing to give up Lily. "Let her sleep."

It only made sense. Kate wasn't too happy, knowing this was temporary. They'd made the mistake of claiming Ben was her fiancé. In a town the size of Wild Oak Canyon, that little tidbit would already have made its rounds.

Kate led the way into the sheriff's office, determined to take charge of this situation, starting with reporting the biker attack.

Deputy Dwayne Schillinger sat in a chair behind a desk, his feet propped on a stack of paper, his hand curled around a burger. "Well, well. To what do we owe the pleasure of your visit so soon?" The man let his boots drop to the floor with a thump and laid his lunch in the wrapper.

"I want to report another attack on my property and a death threat," Kate said.

"What kind of attack might that be?" Dwayne wiped his hands down the sides of his uniform, leaving a streak of yellow mustard. He finally pushed out of his chair and stood.

"A gang of bikers rode through my yard, attacked Ben and damaged property. As they left, they shouted out a death threat."

"Can you describe the men?"

"They wore bandannas around their faces and they rode motorcycles." Kate's fists clenched. "I think they were Hispanic."

"That's not much to go on. Without more detailed physical descriptions, I can't go out and arrest anyone. You have to do a little better than that."

Kate let out a frustrated huff. "Don't you know the people of this county? There can't be that many and surely you know who owns motorcycles and who doesn't."

Ben stepped up beside Kate and added softly, "One of the men had a tattoo of a snake. It wrapped around his wrist and forearm."

"Now *that* I might be able to do something with. Sounds like Guillermo Ramirez. His friends call him Snake."

A shred of relief rippled through Kate. A name for her attacker was better than nothing. "I suggest you arrest him for trespassing and assault."

"As soon as I can find him. Like his nickname, he's pretty slippery and difficult to track."

Kate fisted her hands on her hips. "I have a child living with me. I don't want this to happen again. Are you going to do your job and track down the man? Or do I need to call in the state police?"

Dwayne patted her arm. "Now, don't get your panties in a wad, young lady. We take our work seriously out here. We'll get right on it."

Kate nodded to the stack of papers on his desk. "Aren't you going to take notes, a statement or anything?"

"Don't need to." He tapped a finger to his temple. "I'll remember."

Kate dragged in a deep breath, closed her eyes and counted to three. "Thank you for caring." She turned and marched toward the door.

As she reached for the knob, the deputy called out, "Wouldn't have to be scared for yourself or your daughter if you weren't living on the Flying K."

Kate spun. "And what's that supposed to mean?"

Deputy Dwayne shrugged. "Nothing good's come of living at the Flying K. Look what happened to your father."

Kate walked back toward the man. "Are you telling me my father didn't die of natural causes like the medical examiner claimed?"

Dwayne's squinty eyes rounded. "No, ma'am. Just saying it ain't a healthy place to raise a family."

"You know something I don't?"

The deputy raised his hands. "No, ma'am. Just saying."

"I suggest you find this Snake guy and arrest him. That would go a long way toward making the Flying K a healthier place to live." Kate left the building.

Ben followed, chuckling. "Nice."

"I don't need your patronization. I need answers." Kate stomped to the truck and yanked on the handle. Her nail bent back for her effort and the door remained closed. "Dang it!"

"Mommy?" Lily's eyes fluttered open. "Why were you yelling at that man?"

All the starch went out of Kate. "Oh, sweetie. I was just a little disappointed with him." Inside she bit hard on her tongue. "A little disappointed" was a huge understatement.

Ben clicked his key fob and the locks on the truck popped up. "Bank next?" His mouth twitched on the corners.

If Kate wasn't mistaken, the man was fighting a smile.

A shot of anger flared and died as she tried to picture her tirade with the deputy from Ben's view. Okay, so it must have been amusing to the man to see a woman dressed in a sundress and sandals rip into Deputy Dwayne with all his self-importance, attitude and mustard tracking down his shirt. "Smile and I'll serve your teeth on a platter," she warned, her own lips quirking upward. After the tension of the night and early morning, she could use a good laugh, even at her own expense.

"I wouldn't dare." Ben settled Lily in her booster seat and stepped back, allowing Kate to buckle her daughter in.

Her mood a little lighter, Kate climbed into the passenger seat and leaned back. "Not the bank yet. I want to go to the county tax assessor's office. There has to be a mistake about my father's back taxes."

Ben drove the three blocks from the sheriff's office to the county offices. When he pulled up in front of the building, he left the engine running. "I have a call to make. Will you be all right on your own for a few minutes?"

"Hopefully Lily and I will be safe inside the county offices. When we're done there, we'll go next door to the bank. Take your time." Kate climbed out, lifted Lily from her seat and took her hand, entering the cool interior of the county offices.

"Can I help you?" An older woman with gray hair and a pair of glasses perched on the end of her nose smiled a greeting.

"I hope you can." Kate pulled the letter from her purse and laid it on the counter. "I need information on the Flying K Ranch and any taxes owed on the place."

The woman grimaced. "Ma'am, I'm sorry but the computer is down and has been for two days now. The technician hasn't been able to fix it and we're waiting on someone from state to help." She pushed a form toward Kate. "If you'd like to fill out this form and leave it with me, I'll check the records as soon as I have access."

Kate sighed. "Thanks." While Lily stood patiently beside her, Kate filled out the form, then showed the woman her driver's license and a copy of the deed to the ranch as proof of ownership.

"Do you know when they'll have the system back up?"

"Not a clue. Check back tomorrow. Hopefully it'll be up then."

"Thank you." Kate left, Lily's hand clasped in hers, no less tense than when she'd entered the building a few minutes earlier. No use obsessing over a downed computer; she had only thirty days to come up with the cash, should she need it. No time like the present to see what the bank could do for her. She entered the cool, brightly lit bank lobby, her shoulders back, a smile pasted on her face.

ONCE THE TWO girls were out of the truck, Ben glanced at his cell phone. Two bars. *Here's hoping.* His cell phone had been such a big part of his life in Austin. Out here in South Texas, he was lucky to use it at all.

He hit the speed dial for Hank Derringer and held his breath, not letting it out until the device sent a ringing sound back to him.

"Howdy, Ben," Hank answered.

"We need to talk."

"I take it you've met Kate?"

"I have." He inhaled and let out the breath before jumping in. "I need you to reassign me."

A long pause met his request.

"Did you hear me?" Ben prompted.

"I did. Only I've already assigned the other three members of CCI to cases." Hank cleared his throat and continued, "Is something wrong with Kate?"

"No. It's just that I'm not the right man for this particular job."

"I have full confidence in your abilities. I didn't choose you for this case by acci—"

"You didn't tell me she had a child." Ben cut him off, not wanting to hear Hank's arguments.

"Ah." That one word said it all.

"I'm not cut out to play bodyguard to this woman and her little girl. You need someone who…that… Well, damn. Get someone else."

"This has to do with Julia and Sarah, doesn't it?" Hank asked softly.

It was Ben's turn to leave dead air between the two of them. He swallowed hard on the giant lump clogging his throat before he could croak out his answer. "Yeah."

"Look, Ben, it was exactly the reason I hired you for this job. You have more of a stake in this case, more of an understanding of what's at risk, than anyone else on the team. I picked the right man."

"I can't do it."

"Yes. You can." Hank's voice softened even more. "I heard about the intruder last night and about the biker gang attack this morning. I wish I could send someone else to help you, but I just don't have the resources yet."

Ben snorted. "Good news travels fast, doesn't it?"

"What can I say? It's a small town and I have a few friends."

"In the meantime I'm stuck, is that what you're telling me?"

"You've met Kate and Lily. You've seen a little of what they're up against. At this point, could you really walk away?" Hank left a pregnant pause for Ben to respond. When he didn't, Hank went on, "I stand by my decision. I think you're the right man for the job."

"So it's take this one or resign?"

"You're not the kind of man to resign, if I read your dossier right."

Damn the man. He'd done his homework. He knew Ben more than Ben knew, or would admit to knowing, himself.

"Is that all you have?" Hank asked.

"No, can you use your connections to run a background check on Larry Sites and Guillermo Ramirez?"

"Had a check done on Larry Sites when the man disappeared after Kendrick's death. Newspapers reported that he was suspected of Kendrick's murder, that he's wanted for questioning. Otherwise, he didn't have an arrest record."

"Know anything about Ramirez? The man has a snake tattoo on his arm. He seemed to be the leader of the biker gang attack."

"I'll get an official background check on him, but from what I know, he's a thug for hire. It's rumored he works for whatever cartel will pay him the most. He's walking a thin line doing that. I'm surprised someone hasn't put a bullet in him yet. Part of it has to do with his ability to disappear. We suspect he slides across the border when it's hot on this side."

"Nice." Ben's fingers tightened on the cell phone. Kate was in a lot more trouble than just a biker gang harassing her. "Let me know when you find my replacement. Until then, I'll do the best I can."

"Thanks, Ben. Kate and Lily need you out there." Hank clicked off.

Ben sat for a long moment, staring at the street, heat waves rising from the asphalt, making mirages rise up before his eyes in wavering images of his dead wife and child.

Maybe it was the heat waves, maybe it was the tears. Ben blinked and Julia and Sarah disappeared.

He fought the urge to step on the accelerator and drive. Out of town, away from this job, from Kate and Lily. Hell, out of Texas altogether.

Instead he placed another call while he still had reception.

"Jenkins speaking."

Ben immediately recognized the voice on the other end of the connection as Detective Jenkins of the Austin Police Department. "Jenkins, Ben Harding here. I need some help."

"Ben? Is that you?" Jenkins pitched his voice low, almost to a whisper. "Man, where are you? As far as anyone knows you fell off the face of the earth."

"I'm in South Texas near a little town called Wild Oak Canyon."

Jenkins chuckled. "I guess it's true, then. You did fall off the face of the earth. What can I do for you?"

Ben jumped in. "Who's handling my case?"

"Man, you know I'm not at liberty—"

"Damn it, Jim. Who's handling it?"

Jenkins sighed. "Masters was assigned after you left."

"Anything new?"

"Not much. I think Masters tracked down the man who supplied the girls to Frank Davis. We don't have much, other than hearsay, so we haven't made an arrest yet."

"Girls?" All he knew about was the one Davis had killed.

"Apparently Davis was more deviant than originally suspected."

Ben's hand tightened around the cell phone. He wanted to kill Davis all over again. "Who was the supplier?" he asked through clenched teeth.

"You know I can't give you that kind of information. You're not on the force anymore."

Ben slammed his palm against the steering wheel. "When did you start following all the rules?"

"When you got fired." His tone was flat, final. "Why do you want to know?"

"I killed a man for killing a girl. I want to know it wasn't in vain. From the sound of it there are more women and girls being trafficked."

The silence on the other end indicated he'd gotten his friend's attention.

"Who supplied the girls to Davis? If they are victims of a human trafficking ring, it has to stop."

"I don't like going against department rules."

"Lives could depend on this." Ben's hand tightened on the receiver as he waited for his friend's response.

"Look, we know that. Masters is working the case."

"So let me help. What's it going to hurt?"

"You, me…I don't know, but I don't like playing both sides of the law."

"I'm no rogue and I doubt I could get into much trouble way down south where I am, but if there's any way I can help, I will."

After a long pause, Jenkins said, "His name is Rolando Gonzalez. He's here in Austin, but we suspect he has connections to the Mexican Mafia. As a matter of fact, he's got family in South Texas. Let me pull the file and get back with you. If you could do some looking around while you're down there, we might get more on him and who he's working for. Just don't do anything stupid."

Like killing him before they could get information out of him? Ben knew he'd gone beyond his limit on Davis. Seeing that girl lying on that cot, beaten, bleeding and past help… Ben stared out the window, his heart racing as if he was there all over again.

A movement on his right jerked him back to the present.

Kate and Lily exited the county tax assessor's office, waved at him and walked next door to the bank. If Hank got him off this case with Kate, he would have time to check out the lead Jenkins was talking about.

"I don't get reception out on the ranch where I'm working, so leave a message on my cell. If it's urgent, contact Hank Derringer." Ben left Hank's number with Jenkins. "I'll be waiting for that information."

"Will do. And Harding…stay safe. If this is as big as I think it is, you don't want to get caught in the cross fire of the Mexican Mafia."

Hell, he couldn't afford to get in the middle of the Mafia, not when he had Kate and Lily to protect. He'd wait to make any inquiries until Hank found a replacement.

"I NEED TO take out an equity loan on my father's—my ranch and open a three-thousand-dollar line of credit until I can withdraw money from a CD I set up for Lily's college." Kate leaned forward, her anger building with each time Art Manning tapped his pen to the loan application form in front of him.

"I'm sorry, Ms. Kendrick."

"Langsdon."

"Ms. Langsdon. I'll have to perform a complete credit check on you and have our corporate underwriters approve this before I can give you an answer. In the meantime I suggest you open an account here. We can't loan money to anyone who is not a current client of our bank."

"I see." Kate stood. In the meantime, she was running low on cash and she needed money to pay Eddy and Ms. Henderson's salaries, not to mention putting food on the table and all the deposits she'd needed to get the electricity and gas switched over to her name.

"While your underwriters are thinking about it, I'll be thinking about whether or not to open an account." She gathered Lily's hand in hers.

"Ms. Kendrick."

"Langsdon."

"Without a job and a current income, I doubt the underwriters will take your application seriously."

"The land isn't enough collateral to secure a mortgage?"

"Not given the history of that particular parcel and its location."

"You mean I won't be able to get a loan?"

He shook his head. "I doubt it."

Kate breathed in and let it out before speaking again. "Thank you for your time, Mr. Manning."

She headed for the door, ready to be out in the heat, away from the stuffy air-conditioned atmosphere of the bank building.

"You look like your father." The voice belonged to a businessman dressed in a tailored suit leaning against the stand containing blank deposit slips.

Kate's steps faltered and she glanced at the man, her eyes narrowing. "Seems to be the consensus. If you'll excuse me…" Impatient and tired after a sleepless night and the fright of the morning, Kate had no intention of stopping to chat and she veered to the side.

The stranger stepped out, blocking her path to the exit. He stuck out his hand. "I'm Robert Sanders. Your father and I were friends."

To avoid being outright rude, Kate clasped the man's hand and shook it briefly. "Nice to meet you, Mr. Sanders. I'm Kate."

"Kate Langsdon." He held on to her hand longer than Kate wanted, then let go. "You have his eyes."

"I thought the hair was the dead giveaway."

"Your father's hair was much darker." Sanders raised a hand to touch one of Kate's curls.

She backed away.

The man's hand fell to his side. "But the green eyes are unmistakably his. I believe your mother had blue eyes, did she not?"

His comment took the wind out of Kate's sails. "You knew my mother?" So far, no one in town had mentioned her mother. Most people she'd run across in Wild Oak Canyon mentioned Kyle Kendrick, but not her mother, as though she'd never been there.

"No, but your father had a picture of his ex-wife on his desk. You don't look much like her at all."

That made Kate smile and her gut twist at the same time. "My mother always said I was a constant reminder of my father."

"Your mother must have been a very special woman. Your father never married after she left."

A spike of anger flared in Kate's gut. She'd loved her mother until the day she'd died. But if she had one regret in her relationship, it was that her mother had chosen to lie to her about her father, claiming he was dead, instead of alive and available if she'd wanted to meet him.

Kate suddenly felt stifled in the bank. "If you'll pardon me." She wanted out. Knowing Ben was waiting made her all the more anxious to leave, ready to get back to safe territory.

That thought gave her pause.

Damn.

After only one day, she'd come to rely on the strength and presence of Ben. If things didn't get better soon, she ran the risk of becoming too dependent on him.

Since her husband's death, Kate had been hesitant to date, unwilling to drag her daughter through relationships that wouldn't last. Not many men wanted to date a woman with a ready-made family.

Not that she wanted to date Ben. But the close proximity of a bodyguard could lead to the same outcome. Lily could become attached.

As she stepped around Mr. Sanders, the man handed her his business card. "I feel somewhat responsible for the well-being of my friend's daughter." When she didn't take his card, he lifted her hand, laid the card in it and curled her fingers around the paper. "Please, if there is anything I can do, don't hesitate to call."

Kate clutched the card. "Thank you." When she turned to leave, his hand caught her elbow.

"If you don't mind, I'd like to visit the ranch and make sure you're doing okay out there all alone."

"That won't be necessary."

"I insist."

"I'm not alone. I have my…fiancé staying with me. I'm quite all right."

Sanders's eyes narrowed fractionally, then his brows rose. "So, wedding bells are in the near future for you, are they?" He grasped her hands again. "Congratulations, my dear. I'm so happy for you."

Kate pulled free of Mr. Sanders's grip. "Thank you." She snatched Lily's little hand and turned away, hating the lies she was telling this town, but feeling more comfortable with the fact that Ben's presence would keep her safe. At least it might make others think before they set foot on her property. The more the people of the county thought a man lived there full-time, the better off she was. A lone woman on a ranch could be considered a target. Especially a ranch in cartel territory.

Houston was looking better every minute. But Kate had come too far to turn back now. She wanted to find out why her father had died. If he hadn't died of natural causes, Kate wanted to know who had killed him and why.

BEN HAD HIS hand on the gearshift ready to pull away from Wild Oak Canyon, to start a new life…elsewhere. As he flexed his arm to move the gear, Kate pushed through the glass doors, leading Lily by the hand, a troubled expression on her face.

Instead of driving away, Ben found himself climbing down and opening the rear passenger door before Kate reached the vehicle. The slump in her shoulders and the dullness in her eyes plucked at his heartstrings more than he cared to admit. "I take it that meeting didn't go well."

"County computers are down until further notice, so I struck out there."

Ben lifted Lily into her seat and buckled her belt. "We can come back tomorrow."

"Then the bank…" Kate stepped on the running board and slid into the passenger seat. "I only asked for a home equity loan to help me catch up in case I owed back taxes, and a line of credit loan to last me long enough so that I can sort through my father's will and cash in some certificates of deposit I have set aside for Lily's college fund." She snorted. "You'd think I'd gone in there asking for a fortune."

Ben didn't trust himself to comment. His insides churned. He didn't want to admit to Kate how close he'd been to leaving her and Lily in Wild Oak Canyon. What kind of coward left a woman and her child to fend for themselves?

Once they were all in the truck and belted, Ben rounded the truck and climbed into the driver's seat.

Kate sighed. "I guess the only good thing out of those two stops is this." She held up a business card. "This Robert Sanders claimed he was a friend of my father's and gave me his card in case I needed anything."

Ben reached for the card. "Let me see that."

Kate handed it over. "Looks legit."

Robert Sanders of Sanders Homes. Real Estate Broker and Construction.

Ben turned the card over, then handed it back to Kate. "Let me have Hank check him out before you get too chummy."

Kate nodded and slid the card into her purse.

Ben would keep an eye out for Sanders. If he really was a friend of Kyle Kendrick, he shouldn't be a threat to Kate. But then Kyle's place hadn't been broken into. He'd known his attacker.

Ben shifted into gear and pulled out onto the road.

"I need to stop at the hardware and feed stores for the things Eddy wanted me to get." Kate pulled a sheet of notepaper from her purse. "He handed it to me on the way out of the house." She glanced over her shoulder at Lily. "Then we can go to the diner and have supper. Would you like that, Lily?"

Lily's eyes widened, a smile lighting her face. "Do they have milk shakes?"

Kate let her daughter's happiness wash over her and she smiled back. "I don't know, but we'll find out."

"Can I have a chocolate milk shake?" Lily's feet bounced on the seat back.

Ben laughed. "We'll see when we get there."

In less than an hour, they had what they needed loaded into the back of the truck.

"Guess it's a good thing *you* drove today. I haven't had the chance to go through my father's barn and see if he had a truck. This ranching thing is all new to me."

"I can help you there."

"I thought you were a bodyguard. Were you a cowboy in your former life?"

"I grew up on a ranch." He'd loved living on a ranch, riding horses and raising cattle. But his family didn't own the ranch. Once his father's health declined to the point he could no longer handle the hard work, they'd moved to Austin where both his parents died in a multicar pileup on the interstate the week after Ben graduated from college.

"So is it true, once a cowboy, always a cowboy?" Kate's question pulled Ben back to the present.

He wasn't looking at her, but he could feel Kate's direct stare, and it made him uncomfortable. Why did she have to ask so many dad-burned questions?

He didn't respond with anything more than a shrug.

Her lips twisted. "Nice to know. You must be a man of many talents. Anything else you'd like to share with me?"

"No." Ben pulled into the parking lot of Cara Jo's Diner. The timing couldn't have been better. He shouldn't have shared anything about his existence before Kate. None of that existed anymore. Not his parents, not his wife and child and not his work as an Austin police officer.

His slate was clean. What he did with his life now was the only thing he could do.

Start over.

A pretty young woman wielding a broom swept the sidewalk in front of the diner and smiled brightly when Ben stepped from the truck. She stopped to reach into a big cardboard box. When she straightened, there was a round-bellied puppy in her arms. "Howdy. I don't suppose ya'll want a puppy."

Kate had just set Lily on her feet and reached back into the truck to retrieve her purse, a hand holding on to the child's.

Lily wiggled free of Kate's grip, squealed and ran for the box. When she tried to step up on the curb, her sandal caught and she tripped, her little body slamming into the sidewalk.

Before Kate could reach her, Lily raised her arms for Ben to pick her up, tears streaming from her eyes.

Ben gathered her in his arms and cradled her. When he glanced up, his gut clenched at the paleness of Kate's face. He tried to pry the little girl's arms from around his neck, but she wouldn't let go. "Don't you want your mama?"

Lily buried her face in his shirt. "No, I want you."

Chapter Seven

Lily's knees and hands were scraped and bleeding. Her big emerald-green eyes filled with tears. "Am I gonna die?"

Ben smiled down at Lily. "No, baby, you'll be just fine."

Kate's heart skipped a few beats. A pang of jealousy tugged at her. But more than that, her chest tightened at how quickly Lily had assimilated Ben into her life. When he left, he'd leave a hole in her daughter's world that Lily wouldn't understand. She wouldn't be fine.

"Let's get her inside." The woman with the broom set the puppy down in the box and leaned her broom against the wall. "I have a first aid kit in the kitchen."

As Ben stepped into the diner, Lily practically crawled over his shoulder. "I want to see the puppies," she cried.

Kate followed Ben. "After we clean up your boo-boos, sweetheart, you can see the puppies."

"Can I hold one?" She sniffled and rubbed her arm over her nose.

Kate handed Lily a tissue from her purse. "If the nice lady says you can."

The broom lady chuckled. "My name's Cara Jo Smithson. And yes, you can hold one."

Lily grinned, her tears disappearing.

"So you're *the* Cara Jo?" Ben asked. "You're not what I expected as the owner."

Cara Jo laughed and batted her eyes. "I hope you mean that in a good way." The diner owner glanced over her shoulder at Ben, her footsteps slowing.

Kate had a sudden urge to scratch Cara Jo's eyes out for flirting with Ben. Then she had to remind herself the engagement was just a big fib. She had no hold on Ben and no right to be jealous if he flirted with the stunning Cara Jo. "The first aid kit?" Kate prompted.

"Oh, yes. This way." The woman marched to the back of the dining room and through a swinging door. Cara Jo held the door for Ben, Lily and Kate. "The washroom is at the rear of the kitchen. The first aid kit is in there under the sink."

Kate assumed the lead, stepping past shiny stainless-steel preparation tables and a huge gas stove.

"Let's get you fixed up." Cara Jo eased past Kate and Ben and entered the employee washroom, where she reached beneath a counter for a large, red plastic container with a big Red Cross sticker plastered to the top.

Ben set Lily on the countertop.

Kate moved to stand beside Ben, her hip so close it rubbed against his. A shot of awareness winged through her and she almost pulled away.

Cara Jo pulled bandages, sterile gauze and an accordion of alcohol prep pads from the kit, handing them to Kate.

While Kate dressed Lily's wounds, Ben distracted the child. He smoothed the red-gold curls out of Lily's face. "How many puppies do you have in that box, Cara Jo?"

Kate smiled, glad Ben's words captured Lily's attention, drawing it away from what Kate was doing.

"There are five, but one is already spoken for."

"What breed are they?"

Cara Jo laughed. "Purebred mutts, as far as I can tell." She opened an alcohol pad and handed it to Kate. "The vet seems to think they're a mix between Australian shepherd and border collie. All I know is that they're fuzzy and cute as can be. I'm having a hard time letting them go. But one dog in the family is enough when I'm working so much here at the diner."

Kate wiped the alcohol pad across Lily's skinned knees.

Lily grimaced and reached for the knee. "Ouch."

Ben caught her hand before she could touch the cleaned wound. "You're doing so well, Lily. I didn't know you were such a big girl. So far, not a single tear."

"Big girls don't cry, do they, Mommy?" Lily darted a look at Kate.

Kate could feel the next sentence coming before her daughter even said it.

"Big girls can take care of puppies, can't they?" Lily's eyes rounded, her head tipping up and down.

Kate's brows furrowed. "I don't know. Puppies are a lot of work. Someone has to feed them every day and take them outside a lot until they learn to go out on their own."

"I can do that." Lily's eyes widened, her bottom lip pouting outward, just a little. "Can I have a puppy, Mommy? Please."

"You just found a kitten. Isn't a kitten enough?" Kate couldn't resist her daughter's sad puppy look. And now that they lived on a ranch, not in an apartment in Houston, she had no excuse. A puppy was a definite possibility. Still, it meant committing fully to living in Wild Oak Canyon. A puppy in a Houston apartment wouldn't work for Kate or the puppy.

"Let Mommy think about it, Lily," Ben said.

"Ben's right." Kate could have kissed Ben, the thought strangely appealing, more so than she wanted to admit. "I need to think about it."

Lily slumped.

"Hey, why the sad face?" Ben chucked a finger beneath her chin. "She didn't say no."

Teardrops shimmered on Lily's eyelashes. "She didn't say yes."

Kate shook her head, smiling. "I want to think about it."

"They'll be ready to wean from their mother any day now," Cara Jo added. "I hope they all have a home soon."

"Based on the one you were holding up before Lily fell, I'm sure they'll be snatched up," Ben said.

A bell jingled from the dining area. "If you two can handle this, I've got a customer. By the way, my special this evening is meat loaf and mashed potatoes, if you plan on staying for dinner."

"We can handle it from here," Ben reassured her. "And yes, we're staying for dinner."

Alone with Ben and Lily in the washroom, Kate's body tingled at the man's nearness. Heck, his broad shoulders practically filled the small space and his strong, capable hands dwarfed hers as he held her daughter.

Fingers fumbling, Kate applied a bandage to the sore knee, then bent and kissed the covered injury. "There, all better."

"Not quite." Ben pulled the rubber band from Lily's ponytail that had been hanging drunkenly to one side. Strands of silky golden-red curls fell loose about her shoulders. "Can't let this brave young lady walk out of here with a lopsided pony." Carefully, he bunched the hair into his hand, smoothing all the lumps, and secured it again in the band.

Kate's breath caught and held throughout the process. Clearly, the man had done this before. She didn't know anything about Ben. For all she knew, he could be married with a little girl of his own. A family he'd soon go home to.

Her stomach flip-flopped, a sense of impending loss leaving an empty space inside. How could this be? The man was nothing more than a hired gun, a bodyguard to protect her. He'd only been around for a day.

Kate had never believed in love at first sight. Not that

what she was feeling was anything like love. Respect, maybe. The man was strong, self-assured and handy to have around in a fight...or fixing a little girl's hair. That pretty much summed up her knowledge of Ben Harding. That, and he'd been a first responder for the Austin Police Department in his past life. What had made him leave to go work for Hank Derringer as a bodyguard for hire? The little bits of information she'd gleaned from the quiet man only made Kate want to learn more.

"Come on." Ben swung Lily up in his arms. "If it's all right with your mother, we'll go see those puppies now."

"I was thinking dinner would be a good idea."

The disappointment on Lily's face made Kate reconsider. "Okay, but only for a few minutes. I'll order our food while you two play with the puppies." She raised questioning brows at Ben. "Anything you'd like in particular?"

For a long moment, he stared down at her, with Lily perched on his arm. His blue eyes smoldered, his gaze lowering to somewhere south of Kate's nose.

Her pulse quickened, her mouth going dry. Kate ran her tongue across suddenly parched lips. "Food...what kind of food would you like?"

His mouth twitched. "Cara Jo's mention of meat loaf and mashed potatoes sounded great. I haven't had meat loaf in a long time."

"Meat loaf it is." Kate couldn't get out of the washroom fast enough. Heat suffused her entire body at the thought of Ben's full lips, that blue-eyed gaze bearing down on her, reminding her she was more than just a mother. She was a young woman with needs and physical desires she'd thought long gone with the death of her husband.

In an attempt to get her ragged breathing under control, Kate sat at one of the empty booths and waited for Ben and Lily to step outside before she dared follow them with her gaze.

"You're one lucky lady." Cara Jo stood at her elbow, a pad and paper in her hand.

"How so?" Kate wasn't feeling so lucky. At the moment, she felt trapped by her own raging hormones and latent desires.

Cara Jo spread her hands, palms up. "Why, your husband, of course."

"Fiancé," Kate corrected.

Cara Jo glanced out the big window at Ben squatting beside the box, handing Lily a puppy. "That man's hot, and he's really good with your daughter."

Kate's gaze followed Cara Jo's. "Yes, he is." Too good with her daughter and too handsome for Kate's own good.

"Let me know if you ever decide to give him up."

"Why?"

"He's just the kind of guy I'm looking for."

Kate's teeth ground together and she fought to keep from saying something stupid like *he's mine, keep your greedy hands off him*. Once again, she had to remind herself that she had no claim on Ben and that he wasn't even her fiancé. "You'll be the first to know," she said through tight lips.

Cara Jo laughed. "Lighten up. I'm not going to steal your man. He's in love with you, not me."

If only.

Kate's eyes widened and she almost jumped up from the table and ran. What the hell was she thinking? Ben wasn't her man. They'd only known each other for a day. He didn't—couldn't—love her and she'd better get such crazy thoughts from her head before she did something even more stupid, like falling for the big guy.

"Are you ordering for yourself or your family?"

"All of us." Kate had let the family comment slip right by so easily without trying to correct Cara Jo. At this point, she couldn't retract the lie without backtracking with the sheriff's office and anyone else who'd spread the rumor.

"So you're the folks who've moved onto the Flying K Ranch? I'm glad."

Kate's gaze shot to Cara Jo's. "You are? Why?"

Cara Jo shrugged with the hint of a smile. "Gets kinda lonesome out here in the middle of nowhere. There's not nearly enough women our age to talk to." Cara Jo's smile widened. "A girl could always use a friend."

Kate's eyes misted. "Thanks. I was feeling a bit overwhelmed by the acres of land between me and my nearest neighbor."

Cara Jo's sunny face darkened. "I hear you had some trouble out your way."

"Someone broke into the house the first night I was there."

"And what's this I heard about a motorcycle gang tearing through your yard?" Cara Jo shook her head. "What's with people? It's as though they're trying to scare you off or something."

"I'm getting that feeling, too. I just don't know why." Kate tipped her head to the side. "Did you know my father?"

"A little. He stopped by the diner for supper occasionally." Cara Jo gazed into Kate's eyes. "You have his eyes. I remember them being a pretty shade of green."

"So people say. I wouldn't know." Kate glanced toward Ben and Lily. "I never met the man."

"Really?" Cara Jo's pretty brow furrowed. "I think he traveled a lot. He never said much when he came in, but he was always polite and tipped well. He had a great smile, but apparently he didn't talk to anyone else about his life or what he was up to on the Flying K. He was a recluse."

"I wonder why he didn't get to know his neighbors."

Cara Jo leaned closer. "Some say he was involved in the Mexican Mafia. I'm usually a good judge of character. I didn't see it in him."

"I wish I'd had the chance to get to know him." Her comment was no more than a whisper.

Cara Jo's frown deepened. "Yeah and if wishes were horses…"

"…beggars would ride," Kate finished.

The diner owner bent toward Kate and hugged her with her free arm. When she straightened, she swiped at moisture in her eyes and laughed. "Hey, what say we do lunch sometime?"

Warmth washed over Kate. Nobody in Houston had volunteered to be her friend. Rarely had she gone out to lunch with anyone other than Lily.

She'd been casual acquaintances with her coworkers at the hobby store where she'd been employed. Scraping out an existence for her and Lily on what little she made and the money from her husband's life insurance became an exhausting job. Spare time was spent with her daughter, going to the parks and zoo.

"I'd love to do lunch." Kate smiled up at Cara Jo. "Maybe you'd like to get out of town and come visit the ranch? I can make a mean grilled cheese sandwich." Kate glanced around the diner. "I'm not a grand cook."

Cara Jo snorted. "And you think I am? I have the usual. If I change things up, I get complaints. People can be such creatures of habit."

"Cara Jo," a gray-haired older man called out from a booth on the other side of the entrance.

"I'll be right with you." Cara Jo grinned. "Don't be surprised if I show up on your doorstep real soon. In the meantime, what's your poison?"

Kate gave her new friend their order and sat back, admiring the tall, curvy young blonde's happy efficiency at handling her customers.

A squeal from outside drew Kate's attention.

Lily squatted on the wooden planks of the front porch, reaching out to a rambunctious black-and-white pup that nipped at her fingers. She jerked her hand away from the dog's sharp teeth and giggled.

Ben sat back on his haunches, smiling at the child. Every once in a while, his smile dimmed and his gaze grew somber.

Kate sat forward, studying the man.

The bodyguard had dark wavy hair hanging down to his collar. His square chin and lean, muscular body spoke of strength and discipline. But those smoky-blue, brooding eyes held too many shadows. Someone or something had hurt this man.

Kate closed her eyes and told herself she didn't want to know who and what had caused him so much pain. She couldn't keep them closed long. Lily squealed again and Ben's rich laughter made her want to go outside and join them.

"You should go see the puppies. They're too cute to miss." Cara Jo was at her side again. The diner owner set three glasses of ice water on the table and utensils wrapped in bright red cloth napkins. "Your food won't be ready for a few minutes. Go on before I do. That man is too yummy to be left alone long."

"No, I'll just wait here." Kate was already too aware of the man and the magnetism that pulled at her.

Lily giggled again, making Kate's heart leap.

"Have it your way, but those puppies will steal your heart." Cara Jo walked away to tend to another customer.

Lily squealed again, and Ben's laughter followed. Unable to resist, Kate rose from the booth seat and pushed through the front door out onto the porch. "Okay, you two are having entirely too much fun. Let's see what you've got."

Ben grinned up at her, the shadows gone from his eyes. "I think Pickles is her favorite."

"And which one is Pickles?" Kate dropped down on her knees and peered into the large cardboard box.

Five fluff balls growled in their puppy voices while tearing at a stuffed toy that had seen better days. Each puppy had its own unique coloring. Three were the mottled gray, white, black and red of the Australian shepherd. Two were black-and-white like a border collie.

In the corner closest to where Lily stood, one of the black-and-white pups leaped against the side of the box.

"Look, Mommy, Pickles has pretty blue eyes." She dangled her hand in the box and Pickles snapped at it, his high-pitched bark playful.

Lily laughed and hid her hand behind her back, looking up at Kate with shining eyes. "Can we take him home? Please, Mommy."

Kate lifted the puppy from the box and held him in the air. The gyrating ball of fur wiggled its way out of her hand. Kate caught Pickles before he hit the ground, her heart lodged in her chest. "You are a mess, little fellow."

"No, he's not. He's happy you picked him." Lily pointed at Pickles's long black tail tipped with white. "See, he's wagging his tail."

Kate held the puppy up to her face. The little fellow licked the air, trying to get her nose, making her laugh at his persistent attempts.

Raised by her mother in a small condo in the city, she'd never been allowed to have a pet. No one was home to take care of it for hours and her mother thought it was unfair to animals to be left alone for so long. That and they could barely afford to put food on their table, much less buy food for a dog.

Kate hugged the puppy to her chest. Closing her eyes, she inhaled the unique scent of puppy fur and puppy breath. The defenseless pup reminded her of a time when she held Lily in her arms, alone in the maternity ward. She'd clung to her baby, after the miracle of her birth, realizing Lily was the only person she had left to love in her world.

Tears welled in her eyes and she blinked to keep them from falling. When she looked up, her gaze met Ben's.

All the pain of her own loneliness shone back to her like a mirror in his eyes.

Ben stood, his jaw tightening until a muscle jerked on one side of his face. "I'll wait in the truck."

Her heart squeezing in her chest, Kate asked, "What about supper?"

"I'm not hungry," he called out without looking back.

Chapter Eight

Ben walked away. He would have run if he thought it would help. But no matter how far he ran, he couldn't escape the image of Kate staring at him through tear-soaked eyes.

As he dropped down off the porch, the sound of Lily's voice reached out to him, slamming another bullet into his heart. Sarah had been that enthusiastic, filled with a beautiful love of life. His daughter had been the joy of his existence.

For a few short minutes, he'd let Lily into his heart, laughing for the first time in two years. Letting her happiness revive his dead heart. Guilt swamped him, dragging him into that bottomless pit he'd crawled into after he'd discovered his wife and daughter murdered in their home.

How could he let another little girl fill that void?

And Kate's tears had touched him like nothing else since Sarah's death. He shouldn't be having these feelings. He'd lost his chance at love. He'd squandered it by not being there to protect them. Instead he'd been chasing his career as a cop, fighting to keep criminals off the street.

Ben jumped into his truck and slammed his door, then he hit the steering wheel with his palm so hard, pain reverberated through his hand and up into his arm. He welcomed it, using it to refocus on why he was there.

He had to regain his self-control or risk the lives of the

people he was there to protect. No matter what, he couldn't let Kate and Lily suffer the same fate as his family.

"Your dinner is ready." Cara Jo appeared in the doorway. Her smile turned into a frown. "Where'd Ben go?"

"He's waiting in the truck. I'm sorry. We're a little tired from all the excitement last night and this morning. Could we get the meal to go?"

"Absolutely. Give me a minute and I'll bring it out."

Kate returned the puppy to the box and then fished in her purse for her wallet, extracting enough cash to pay Cara Jo for the food and a tip. "I don't need any change."

"Honey, consider it my gift to the new girl in town."

"I insist. This is your livelihood." Kate placed the money in Cara Jo's hand and closed her fingers around it. "Please."

Perhaps the other woman saw the moisture in Kate's eyes, because she didn't press the issue. "Okay. Give me a minute."

A couple minutes later, she returned with a bag filled with take-out boxes. The heady scent of hot food wafted beneath Kate's nose and her belly growled. "Thank you. And please, come out whenever you'd like."

Lily stared down into the box, her lip trembling. "Can we take him home?" She looked up at Kate, pressing her hands together like she was praying.

"Not today, sweetie. Pickles has to stay with his mommy for a few more days."

"Then can we bring him home?"

"If he's not one of the puppies Ms. Cara Jo has promised to someone else."

Lily's gaze shifted to Cara Jo. "Can I have that one?" She pointed to Pickles, who'd resumed jumping against the side of the box, barking at Lily.

Cara Jo smiled. "You're in luck. He's still available."

Lily squealed and jumped up and down.

Anxious to leave and find out what had made Ben depart

so abruptly, Kate reached out and hugged Cara Jo. "Thanks for everything. I look forward to seeing you soon."

Cara Jo patted her back. "Let me know if I need to bring my shotgun out with me. You stay safe."

Kate slid her purse strap up over her shoulder. One hand held on to the bag of food while the other grabbed Lily's little fingers. "Come on, it's time to go home."

Ben stood beside the truck, his head bent, his hat tipped low, shading his eyes.

As soon as she stepped off the porch, he opened the back door and swung Lily up into her booster seat, buckling her in place. Wordlessly, he took the bag from Kate and settled it on the back floorboard, out of range of Lily's swinging legs.

Kate climbed into the front passenger seat and closed the door, unsure how to broach the subject of his sudden retreat.

When Ben slid in behind the wheel, he didn't look at her; instead he backed away from the diner and headed out of town on the highway leading to the Flying K Ranch.

"Just so you know, I asked Hank to find a replacement for me." His soft-spoken words took a moment to register.

When they did, Kate's head jerked toward him, her heart hitting the bottom of her stomach. "Why?"

"I'm not the right man for this job."

After the craziness of the day, the invasion of her home by a faceless man and the biker gang threats, Ben's announcement scared her the most. Tremors rippled through her body. A chill that had nothing to do with the truck's air-conditioning wrapped around her and she shook uncontrollably. Keeping her voice as even as possible, she remarked in a tone she hoped sounded unconcerned, "You've done pretty darned good so far."

"Nevertheless, when he's got someone else lined up, I'll be leaving."

What could she say to that? Her logical left brain said to

leave it, nothing she could say would convince him to stay if he really wanted to go.

Her emotional right brain urged her to beg him to stay. He'd saved her more than once and she trusted him to do it again.

Instead, she whispered into the darkness, "Why did you walk away from Lily, me and the puppies?"

At first she didn't think he'd heard her and she let it go. Maybe she didn't want to know after all. What if he answered that he didn't like children or that he didn't like her? Nothing made sense. The way he'd been so happy and laughing with Lily led Kate to believe he liked children.

"I couldn't handle it." Ben's words broke through the frigid darkness.

Her heart already strained from his announcement that he'd be leaving; Kate wanted to know more than he was giving her. First she glanced over her shoulder at Lily.

Her baby's head dipped toward her chest, her eyes closed, chest rising and falling in deep, even breaths. Blessedly asleep, unaware of Ben's announcement that he'd be leaving.

Anger cleared Kate's head and forced her to sit up straighter. "Just what is it that you couldn't handle? Is it the constant threats out at the ranch?"

He didn't answer, ratcheting up Kate's annoyance with him for his vagueness and her desire to get to the bottom of the issues.

"Is it me? Am I too demanding?"

He shot a glance at her. "No, it's not you."

"Does Lily have you running scared? I can see that. Most four-year-old children terrify me. Especially ones who idolize me and dog my every step."

Ben's lips curled on the corners in a hint of a smile that never reached his eyes. The light from the dash didn't reflect in their dark depths. "No, Lily is a beautiful little girl."

Kate sucked in a deep breath and let it out between

clenched teeth. "If it's not the situation and it's not me or Lily, what the hell had you running?"

Another long pause lasted a couple miles.

Kate turned away from Ben and stared out at the darkness. Only she couldn't see past the glass reflecting her image and Ben's behind her.

The man stared straight ahead, his eyes smoky dark, the shadows beneath them deep and disturbing.

"I lost people I loved." His voice was agonizingly deep, and the words spoken so softly Kate thought she'd imagined it.

She turned toward him, studying his face. Had he spoken or had she imagined the words?

His hands gripped the steering wheel so tightly his knuckles had turned white. That and a tick in his jaw were the only indications of something going on more than him driving the truck.

"Who did you lose?" Kate asked, daring to believe she'd heard correctly.

"My wife and daughter. Sarah was Lily's age when she and Julia were murdered."

All the air left Kate's lungs and a weight settled on her chest that crushed the will from her. Julia. The name he'd called her when he'd kissed her. "Oh, God. I didn't know." She reached out and touched a hand to his arm.

Being with Lily had to be killing him.

Kate's worst nightmares had been those where she'd lost Lily, but every time she'd awakened to realize it had only been a bad dream.

Ben had lived it.

Her stomach roiled, the pain of loss almost as palpable as if she'd lost Lily. She swallowed hard on the giant lump choking her throat. "I'm sorry." Kate's voice caught on a sob. She looked back at Lily, counting her blessings, knowing that every minute she had with her little girl was precious.

Ben didn't have that anymore. His Sarah was gone.

Her bodyguard, the man who'd protected her and Lily, drove on as if he hadn't spoken at all. His face inscrutable, his lips pulled into a tight line.

As they turned off the highway onto the road that led to the Flying K Ranch, movement caught Kate's attention out of the corner of her eye. Before she could react, something hit the passenger-side door with the force of a freight train, flinging Kate sideways. If not for the seat belt, she'd have slammed into Ben and possibly gone through his window.

Lily screamed from the backseat as the truck lurched sideways and skidded across the road toward the ditch.

Ben fought to keep the vehicle on the pavement, but the driver's-side tires bit into the shoulder before he could right the vehicle.

Kate barely had time to straighten before the truck was hit again. All she could see before she was tossed against the restraining belt was a dark grille and the glass of headlights that hadn't been turned on.

Ben cursed, grinding his foot to the accelerator, trying to get away from their attacker. The impact pushed them off the road and down into the ditch so fast the truck teetered on two wheels.

Her breath caught in her throat as the truck wavered, then dropped to all four tires, the jolt flinging her against the door.

Lily cried out.

"Hold on, baby," Kate called out.

Switching the truck into four-wheel drive, Ben gunned the gas pedal. The tires slipped on the gravel, then the knobby treads dug into the dirt and the truck shot back out onto the road.

The dark, steel-gray haze of dusk surrounded them.

Kate twisted in her seat, peering into the semi-darkness of a cloudy starless evening. Behind them, taillights gleamed, two specks of red racing back toward Wild Oak Canyon.

Lily cried softly in the backseat.

The danger past for a moment, Kate unbuckled her belt and crawled over the front seat into the back.

Ben flipped the overhead light on. "Is she all right?" He drove slowly toward the ranch, his gaze darting to the rear-view mirror.

Kate cupped her daughter's face.

Other than silent tears trailing down her cheeks, Lily appeared to be okay. "We're okay, aren't we, baby?"

"Want me to take you two back to town?" Ben offered. "We could report in to the sheriff's office and let him know what happened."

"No. I don't want to risk being out of the vehicle if that guy returns. I just want to go home." She sat in the middle of the backseat beside Lily, holding her child's hand. Soon the tears stopped and Lily fell back to sleep.

Kate trembled in the darkness, afraid of staying where someone obviously didn't want her. She was pissed off that she was being forced out by thugs.

When they arrived at the ranch, Kate unbuckled Lily.

Ben opened the door from the outside and draped Lily's sleeping body over his shoulder.

Kate dropped to the ground, her body stiff from being hurled around the interior of the cab. Her shoulders were sore and her right breast was tender from the force of her body hitting the shoulder strap of her seat belt.

While Ben carried Lily into the house and up the stairs to her bedroom, Kate went from room to room, switching on the lights. When she reached the kitchen, her hand paused on the light switch.

A noise in the pantry captured her attention.

A moment before, she'd been so tired she could barely stand. In an instant, she was on alert. She flipped the light switch on and grabbed for the broom she'd propped beside the door early that morning.

She waited for the next sound that would indicate where the intruder stood.

Her teeth clamped down hard on her lip to keep her from screaming.

A loud click sounded from the pantry and the lights blinked out.

"Kate?" Ben called out from the staircase behind her.

Kate flipped the light switch and nothing happened.

Then something moved in the direction of the walk-in pantry. A door thumped open and footsteps scuffled across the tile.

"Stop or I'll shoot." Kate held the broom up like a shotgun. Her eyes had yet to adjust to the darkness. All she could make out was a shadowy form.

"Then shoot," a voice called out. He lunged for the back door and ran out before Kate could do anything.

And what could she have done? The broom wasn't a gun. At best she could have thrown it at him. At least he hadn't attacked her.

"Kate!" Ben's voice echoed in the living room. "Where are you?"

"In the kitchen. I'm okay."

"What happened?" Footsteps sounded on the wood floor in the hallway and Ben skidded to a halt behind her, his hands reaching out to gather her into his arms. Ben crushed her to his chest. "You scared the hell out of me. Why didn't you answer me the first time?"

"We had an intruder in here. I didn't want him to know where I was."

"Are you all right?"

"I'm fine." *Now that you're here.* She leaned back against him, wrapping his arms securely around her middle.

He turned her in his embrace and tipped her chin up.

Already her eyes were adjusting to the limited lighting. A

soft blue glow poured in through a nearby window as clouds skittered across the sky, freeing the moonlight.

Kate stared up into Ben's dark eyes. "Why is this happening?"

"I don't know." He smoothed a hand over her cheek and it found its way to the back of her neck. He tugged her hair, tipping her head backward, making her lips more accessible to his…kiss.

Ben's mouth closed over hers, sending wave after wave of sensations rippling through Kate's body.

Her hands climbed up his chest, twining around his neck. She applied pressure, wanting more, needing him to deepen their connection, to warm her body with his. To chase away the shadows of fear making her tremble.

His tongue twined with hers, thrusting deep, sliding long and slow, in and out.

When his hands slipped downward, over her shoulder blades and to the small of her back, she didn't protest, couldn't tell him to stop. Not when all she wanted was for him to shove her up against a wall, wrap her legs around his waist and drive deep inside her.

How long had it been since she'd made love to a man? Since before Troy had left for war. Almost five years. More than any woman should have to grieve.

Ben's MEMBER STRAINED against the stiff denim of his jeans, pushing against the button fly, waging a war for freedom. His hand tangled in Kate's thick, lush curls, cupping the back of her head as he bent her over his arm and took what he wanted in the form of a kiss. But it wasn't enough.

The lingering shock waves of adrenaline pulsed through his system, urging him to take action. With no enemy to attack and no imminent danger, his relief could only be derived from making mad, passionate love to this woman whose body warmed his hands and awakened desires long buried.

Kate melted against him; her hands smoothed down the back of his neck and then squeezed between their chests. Her fingers searched for the buttons on his shirt, opening one after the other until she slipped through the opening and touched his skin.

Cool, slim fingers set off a string of explosions inside Ben, sparking nerve endings to life.

Before long, she had all his buttons undone and was tugging his shirt out of his waistband.

Ben found the hem of her dress and pulled it up over her head, tossing the garment to the floor. A black lace bra was all that stood between him and her perfectly rounded breasts.

When her hands locked on the top button of his jeans, his heart skipped several beats and he sucked in a raw, ragged breath.

He closed his hands over hers. "No."

She froze and glanced up, her green eyes shadowed. Then her chin dipped and she backed away. "You're right. I shouldn't have done that. I'm sorry."

Ben's hands fell to his sides, regret burning in his gut. He couldn't let himself be distracted, not with Kate's and Lily's lives at stake. He reached around the wall, feeling for the light switch, and flipped it.

Nothing.

"Know where the breaker box is?" he asked.

"I saw it in the pantry earlier today. The intruder must have known where to look because that's where he was hiding."

"This has got to end." Ben felt his way through the kitchen to the pantry he recalled from unloading Kate's furniture and supplies. There was a sound of rustling fabric, a drawer opened and closed behind him and a beam of light clicked on.

"This might help." Kate, now redressed, followed him into the closet-size room and shone the light on the breaker box. Her presence in the tight confines of the tiny space lined with canned vegetables and boxes of cereal only made matters worse.

He was so tense, he fumbled with the handle to the breaker box before he could get it open and find the tripped switch.

Once the switch had been returned to the on position, light poured through the open pantry door.

Kate backed out, turning off the flashlight. "Just so you know, there are several flashlights in the drawer at the end of the counter here." She slid the electric torch into the drawer and closed it, her hands shaking.

Her gaze slipped up to his, her eyes wide and haunted. "I won't attack you again. I promise."

Ben leaned in the door frame of the pantry. "You didn't attack me. If anything, I was all over you. I've never wanted to kiss someone as much as I wanted to kiss you."

Her brow furrowed. "Then why...?"

"It's wrong. I won't be here long and I don't want to lead you on in any way."

She nodded. "Good, because I'm not in the market for a man. I only need a bodyguard. I don't know what came over me. Must have been the adrenaline rush. Don't worry. I'll leave you alone."

When she turned to leave, Ben shot forward and captured her arm. "Don't get me wrong." He lifted her chin and stared down into her flashing green eyes. "I wanted to kiss you. And I still do." He bent until his lips barely touched hers.

Kate's gaze caressed his mouth, then her eyes rounded and she backed away, spun and ran up the stairs.

It took every ounce of Ben's self-control not to follow her.

Chapter Nine

After lying awake in her bed with her eyes wide open and her mind spinning until the early hours of the morning, Kate finally fell into an exhausted sleep.

Not until Lily skipped into her room the next morning did she open her eyes and squint at the sun shining through her window.

"Oh, baby. I should be up by now to fix your breakfast."

"Mrs. Henderson fixed it for me."

Kate sat up, the T-shirt she'd slept in bunched around her. "She did?"

"Uh-huh. Can I go outside and play?"

Before her daughter finished her sentence, Kate was shaking her head. "Not until I'm up and dressed. You're not to go outside without me or Mr. Harding. Do you understand?"

Lily sighed and crawled up on the bed. "Could you hurry? I saw a lizard on the front porch."

Kate ruffled Lily's strawberry-blond curls. "No rest for the weary, is it? Okay, okay. I'm getting up. Why don't you go down and help Mrs. Henderson in the kitchen?"

"Okay." Lily rolled to the edge of the bed and dropped onto the floor.

The patter of her feet warmed Kate's heart and made her want to get out of bed and join the day.

The fear of the night before faded with the steady heat of the midmorning sun.

She quickly brushed her hair, secured it in a low pony-tail at the base of her head and washed her face. A glance at her wan complexion in the mirror triggered her to dig in the drawer full of cosmetics for powder, blush and a little mascara. No sense looking like death.

Not when there was a handsome man close by. One who'd admitted to wanting to kiss her.

Excitement filtered through her body as she thrust her feet into jeans and pulled them up over her hips. A soft rose T-shirt and pointed-toed pink leather cowboy boots completed her outfit. She hurried from the room and down the stairs to the kitchen, peeking into the living room and ranch office on the way. If she were honest with herself, she'd admit she was looking for Ben.

"He's outside in the yard with Lily," Marge said as she appeared at the kitchen door.

Kate started. Having another person in the house took some getting used to. "I was looking for Lily."

"She's out there with Mr. Harding. They are too cute together. He's hangin' a tire swing for her. Eddy's out rounding up strays. We got here two hours ago."

Kate peered out the window over the kitchen sink at the man hanging from a tree branch. He expertly tied a rope to the branch, then swung out of the tree to land on his feet beside the four-year-old.

Lily grinned up at him, clapped her hands and giggled. "Do it again, Mr. Ben. Do it again," she cried, loud enough Kate could hear her muffled words through the window.

"He scrubbed an old tire he found out back with a brush and dish soap and he found a length of rope in the shed." Mrs. Henderson dried a pan as she gazed out the window, a smile lifting the corners of her mouth.

The image of the man and child made Kate's heart ache.

Lily really needed a father figure. She needed a man in her life to teach her to be adventurous, to show her how to make things and climb trees.

Kate chuckled. Not that the child hadn't learned something about tree-climbing on her own. Kate's smile faded. And thank goodness she had. No telling what the biker gang would have done had they found her outside alone.

A chill shook Kate's body.

"Got a plate of scrambled eggs warming in the oven. Sit yourself down while I pop bread in the toaster."

Kate sank into a chair at the big kitchen table. "You don't have to go to the trouble."

"Now, don't argue with me. I like doin' for others. Makes me feel useful. Oh, by the way, your telephone is working now."

Kate hopped out of her seat. "Good, I want to call the sheriff."

"Oh, honey, I heard about your intruder last night. Ben— Mr. Harding already put a call into the sheriff's office reporting the incident. He said they were sending a deputy out today to look around."

Dropping down to the seat, Kate shook her head. The man was always a step ahead of her.

Marge continued talking as she scooped eggs onto a plate and set it in front of Kate. "I checked around to see if anything had been taken. I could swear I had several cans of soup and tuna I'd planned on using for lunch today. And the loaf of bread I'd laid out was gone." She shook her head. "Looked to me like someone who was hungry slipped in and took what they needed."

"Why wouldn't that person just knock on the door and ask for food? Why steal it?"

"Could have been undocumented immigrants." Marge's brows dipped. "Sometimes a steer will go missing. No telling what's been taken since Mr. Kendrick passed. Eddy said the cattle are all over the ranch. It'll take him days to account for what's left of the herd."

"I suppose I could learn to help him. Do you think Lily would be all right out riding along with us?" Kate had ridden horses a couple times, but she was by no means an expert. Lily had never had the opportunity.

"I could keep her here with me. I'm sure we could find plenty for her to play with around the house."

"I don't want to be a bother."

"No bother. I love little ones." Mrs. Henderson set a glass of orange juice beside Kate's plate. "Eat now. Better to make your decisions on a full stomach."

Kate ate the scrambled eggs and toast, enjoying being waited on for the first time since her mother died. She carried her plate to the sink and ran it through the warm soapy water Mrs. Henderson had used to clean the dishes. No dishwasher in this house.

"Look, he's got the tire up." Mrs. Henderson pointed out the window.

Lily lay on her belly through the hole of the old tire, swinging and laughing out loud.

Her happiness made Kate's heart lighter. She deserved to have a yard to play in and a real home, not an apartment in a busy city.

What would it take to find the ones responsible for trying to run them off the property? Kate wanted a place to call home, for herself as much as she wanted it for Lily. This ranch was the only thing her father had ever given to her, and she'd be damned if she let anyone take it away.

Determination and a sense of purpose flowed through her veins, giving her the inspiration she needed to fight for what she wanted for her and her baby. "Mrs. Henderson, do you know the number for Cara Jo's Diner?"

"Sure do."

Kate called her new friend Cara Jo. Then she brushed

her teeth, stopped in her bedroom for her pistol and a box of ammunition. She shoved the box into her pocket. She held the pistol behind her back, then headed outside to fulfill her promise to herself.

Ben lifted Lily out of the tire and set her on the ground.

Her hair was falling out of her ponytail and she wore a thin coating of dust and a smile. "That was fun. Can we do it again?"

"After a while, sweetie." Kate dropped a kiss on her tousled hair. "Right now, I want you to go inside and help Mrs. Henderson bake cookies."

Lily squealed and ran for the house.

Kate inhaled and let out her breath in a slow, steadying release. "I want to take you up on that offer."

Ben's gaze dropped to her lips. "What offer?"

Heat spread throughout Kate's body at the thought of Ben's kiss. She shoved the image aside and squared her shoulders. "I want you to teach me to shoot my gun." She pulled the weapon from behind her back and held it out.

Ben touched a finger to the tip of the barrel and pointed it away from him. "You start by never pointing a gun at someone unless you want to shoot them."

"It's not loaded." She dug the box of ammo from her jeans pocket and held it out in her other hand.

"Trust me. Make it habit not to point a gun at anyone, loaded or unloaded, unless you intend to shoot him."

"Okay."

Ben took the weapon from her hands and inspected it. "Do you own cleaning supplies for this?"

"Yes."

"Good, it looks good for now, but after we shoot, it'll have to be thoroughly cleaned." He tipped it back and forth and weighted it in his grip. "It's a nice 9 mm Glock. Where did you get it?"

"It was my husband's." She'd almost made him get rid of

it when she'd discovered she was pregnant. After his death, she couldn't bring herself to sell it. Now she was glad she hadn't. "Is it a good brand of gun?" she asked.

"One of the best." Ben clicked a button and the magazine dropped out of the handle. He caught it with his other hand. "Let me see the rounds."

Kate plunked the ammo box in his open palm, careful not to touch him, afraid to set off another bout of uncontrollable lust. That would be a disaster, considering he didn't want anything to do with her. Hadn't he said he was leaving as soon as Derringer arranged a replacement?

Ben loaded the bullets into the magazine. "Make sure your bullets are pointing toward the barrel of the weapon." He showed her how to slip the magazine into the handle and how to release it. Then he handed the gun to her. "You do it."

She didn't care how basic the lessons were, she wanted to learn and get it right the first time. When Ben left, Kate's and Lily's lives depended on Kate's ability to protect them.

Kate held the weapon, searching for the magazine release button. When she found it, she released the magazine and it fell to the ground.

"You'll want to keep your weapon as clean as possible." Ben chuckled, the sound warming Kate's insides.

As Kate bent to retrieve the magazine, a vehicle rumbled down the gravel drive, stirring up a cloud of dust.

"Must be the sheriff's deputy." Ben took the Glock from her and reassembled it, stuffing it into the back of his waistband.

The SUV pulled to a stop. The cloud of dust drifted to the ground and Deputy Schillinger climbed out. "I hear you had another intruder."

"We did," Kate responded. "He was here when we got home after dark yesterday."

Schillinger had a lump of tobacco stuffed between his

teeth and his lower lip. He spit a dark stream of nasty juice on the ground at Kate's feet. "Did you see who it was?"

Kate stepped backward, her breakfast roiling in her gut. "No, he didn't happen to announce himself or show his face. He did get away with some pantry staples and bread."

"Probably illegals."

When Schillinger looked like he would spit again, Kate frowned. "Do you mind?"

The man paused, then let loose anyway, wiping a dark drop from his chin. "Not at all."

Kate stared at the mess on the ground and back at the deputy, then crossed her arms. "And let me guess...you can't do anything without a full description." Kate let out a tight breath. "I don't know why we bother to call you. I'll turn this over to the Customs and Border Protection guys. Maybe they will do something. Thank you for your time."

Another vehicle approached. It slid in beside the deputy's SUV and Cara Jo's long, lithe form stepped out. "Hi, Kate. Got a surprise for Lily." Cara Jo pushed her shoulder-length blond hair back behind her ears, opened the back door and reached in, extracting a black-and-white puppy from the backseat.

Lily burst from the house, racing toward Cara Jo. "It's Pickles! It's Pickles!" She skidded to a stop in the gravel and reached up.

Cara Jo laughed and handed her the puppy. "You have to be very careful with puppies. They're smaller than us and can be hurt easily."

"I'll be very careful. I promise." Lily clutched the squirming puppy against her chest and ran to Kate's side. "Look, Mommy, Pickles is here."

"That's great, honey. Can you take him in the kitchen and get Mrs. Henderson to help find feeding bowls? You can get one of the boxes we used to pack and use it for his bed."

Lily ran toward the house, the puppy flopping in her arms.

Cara Jo joined the group of adults. "What's happening?" She glanced at the deputy. "What are you doing here, Dwayne?"

Kate could have laughed at the way the deputy's lips thinned at being called by his first name. "I was called in on business." His chest puffed out a bit more and he looked down his nose at Kate's new friend.

Cara Jo's brows rose and she turned to Kate. "Business?"

"Unfortunately, the sheriff's department is better at serving papers than they are at finding intruders." Kate gave the lawman a pointed look. "If you're not going to dust for prints or at least write down a statement, I see no further need of your services."

Dwayne's eyes narrowed. "This isn't the place for a woman. You really should consider selling before the bank takes the ranch."

"The bank's not taking anything." She didn't know how, but she'd find a way to come up with some money.

"Then you might want to leave before anything bad happens to you or your little girl."

Ben slipped an arm around Kate's waist. "She's not going anywhere she doesn't want to."

"Besides, it's ridiculous to even consider leaving," Cara Jo said with a snort. "Give up a ranch because the sheriff's department is too scared or lazy to do anything about the growing crime rate in the county?" She hooked Kate's arm and stared at the deputy. "Why are you on the force if you can't do your job?"

Dwayne's face bloomed a ruddy red, his eyes narrowing at Cara Jo. He shifted his attention to Kate. "Think about it, Ms. Langsdon."

Ben's arm dropped from around Kate's waist and he stepped toward the deputy, his fists clenched.

Kate grabbed his hand and slipped it back around her. "He's not worth it."

Schillinger turned and marched to his SUV, climbed behind the wheel and spun out in the gravel on his way out of the drive.

"That man always has a sour look on his face," Cara Jo remarked.

Kate laughed. "I thought it was just me."

"No, it's definitely him." Ben brushed a lock of Kate's hair back behind her ear.

"Thanks for being here for me." Even if Derringer had sent him, Ben had gone above and beyond on more than one occasion. Kate couldn't imagine having to deal with everything that had happened on her own.

"I need to make a call. You going to be all right for a few minutes?" He gazed into her eyes.

Her heart flipped at the worry reflected in his eyes. "I'm fine. Cara Jo's here."

"Go on. We need time for girl talk." Cara Jo waved Ben toward the house.

Once he left them, Cara Jo faced Kate. "Now, what's this about the county foreclosing on your ranch?"

Kate shook her head. "You don't want to know."

"I wouldn't have asked if I didn't care." Cara Jo touched a hand to Kate's arm.

Cara Jo had it right, Kate had needed someone she could talk with and Ben wasn't necessarily the right person. He was the hired help. He couldn't dig her out of her financial hole. Nor did she want him to. She dragged in a deep breath and let it out. "The sheriff and Deputy Schillinger served me with papers that the county is going to seize the property for almost thirty thousand in back taxes."

"Holy moley." Cara Jo flattened a hand to her chest. "That's a lot of cash."

"Yeah." Saying the amount out loud made it sink in all the more, threatening to overwhelm Kate. "I just need time to figure things out. Hire a lawyer or something. But the local bank probably won't loan me any money to keep things going in the meantime."

"I've got a loan on my diner through that bank. But then I grew up here. They know me."

Kate sighed. "I'm an unknown and not a very safe bet." She glanced around at the barn and outbuildings. "And I'm sure the rumors about the attacks aren't giving the bank faith in my abilities to run a ranch and protect my interests."

"You can't help that someone is attacking you." Cara Jo nodded toward where Ben had been. "And you have your fiancé living here. Ben looks fully capable of handling any difficulty."

"Having Ben here didn't help me one bit in the eyes of the bank loan officer." Kate snorted. "I don't even have enough to pay Eddy and Marge until I can get my hands on my daughter's college fund."

"How much do you need?" Cara Jo propped her hands on her hips. "I can't afford thirty thousand, but I can spot you some money until you can get to yours."

Kate's chest swelled, her eyes filling. "No, I can't take advantage of you like that. You barely know me. I'll figure things out. Heck, I've only been here a couple days. Things are bound to get better."

"Sometimes things get worse before they get better. But then, don't let me be the downer here." Cara Jo hugged Kate. "The offer's open if you need it."

"Thanks." Kate gave her a watery smile. "I'll wait and see what the county assessor says when the computers come up again. No use borrowing trouble. I have enough as it is."

FROM THE HALLWAY where the phone was located, Ben could keep an eye on Kate and Cara Jo outside. He dialed Derringer.

"Hank, Ben here."

YOUR PARTICIPATION IS REQUESTED!

Dear Reader,

Since you are a lover of romance fiction – we would like to get to know you!

Inside you will find a short Reader's Survey. Sharing your answers with us will help our editorial staff understand who you are and what activities you enjoy.

To thank you for your participation, we would like to send you 2 books and 2 gifts – **ABSOLUTELY FREE!**

Enjoy your gifts with our appreciation,

Pam Powers

SEE INSIDE FOR READER'S SURVEY

For Your Romance Reading Pleasure...

FREE!

We'll send you 2 books and 2 gifts
ABSOLUTELY FREE
just for completing our Reader's Survey!

YOUR READER'S SURVEY
"THANK YOU" FREE GIFTS INCLUDE:
- ▶ 2 Harlequin Intrigue® books
- ▶ 2 lovely surprise gifts

PLEASE FILL IN THE CIRCLES COMPLETELY TO RESPOND

1) What type of fiction books do you enjoy reading? (Check all that apply)
- ○ Suspense/Thrillers ○ Action/Adventure ○ Modern-day Romances
- ○ Historical Romance ○ Humour ○ Paranormal Romance

2) What attracted you most to the last fiction book you purchased on impulse?
- ○ The Title ○ The Cover ○ The Author ○ The Story

3) What is usually the greatest influencer when you <u>plan</u> to buy a book?
- ○ Advertising ○ Referral ○ Book Review

4) How often do you access the internet?
- ○ Daily ○ Weekly ○ Monthly ○ Rarely or never.

5) How many NEW paperback fiction novels have you purchased in the past 3 months?
- ○ 0 - 2 ○ 3 - 6 ○ 7 or more

YES! I have completed the Reader's Survey. Please send me the 2 FREE books and 2 FREE gifts (gifts are worth about $10) for which I qualify. I understand that I am under no obligation to purchase any books, as explained on the back of this card.

❏ I prefer the regular-print edition   ❏ I prefer the larger-print edition
182/382 HDL F5EY   199/399 HDL F5EY

FIRST NAME	LAST NAME

ADDRESS

APT.#	CITY

STATE/PROV.   ZIP/POSTAL CODE

Printed in the U.S.A.
© 2013 HARLEQUIN ENTERPRISES LIMITED
® and ™ are trademarks owned and used by the trademark owner and/or its licensee.
HI-SUR-07/13

♦ HARLEQUIN® READER SERVICE—Here's How It Works:

Accepting your 2 free books and 2 free gifts (gifts valued at approximately $10.00) places you under no obligation to buy anything. You may keep the books and gifts and return the shipping statement marked "cancel." If you do not cancel, about a month later we'll send you 6 additional books and bill you just $4.74 each for the regular-print edition or $5.49 each for the larger-print edition in the U.S. or $5.24 each for the regular-print edition or $5.99 each for the larger-print edition in Canada. That is a savings of at least 13% off the cover price. It's quite a bargain! Shipping and handling is just 50¢ per book in the U.S. and 75¢ per book in Canada.* You may cancel at any time, but if you choose to continue, every month we'll send you 6 more books, which you may either purchase at the discount price or return to us and cancel your subscription.

*Terms and prices subject to change without notice. Prices do not include applicable taxes. Sales tax applicable in N.Y. Canadian residents will be charged applicable taxes. Offer not valid in Quebec. Books received may not be as shown. All orders subject to credit approval. Credit or debit balances in a customer's account(s) may be offset by any other outstanding balance owed by or to the customer. Please allow 4 to 6 weeks for delivery. Offer available while quantities last.

"Got the phone line hooked up at the Flying K, did you?" Hank asked.

"It's working."

"Good. Had some news on that DVD you sent to me. My contacts in the state crime lab may just be able to recover what was on it. They told me they should have it by this evening. Whatcha got?"

Ben watched as Kate and Cara Jo hugged. What were they talking about? "Can you do some digging on Deputy Dwayne Schillinger and a Mr. Robert Sanders?"

"Why?"

"Schillinger's been out here twice to investigate break-ins, and done nothing but warn Kate to leave."

"Hmm. That doesn't sound right."

"That's what I'm thinking."

"I'll get my contacts on the deputy. I take it you had another break-in last night?"

Ben's hand tightened on the receiver. "We did."

"Anyone hurt?" Hank asked.

"No, he left without attacking."

"As for Robert Sanders, he's pretty well-known in the area, what with his ties to real estate and construction. But I'll have my folks do a little digging to see if he's got any dirt hiding under his rug."

The pounding of horse hooves made Ben glance toward the south. "Hank, I gotta go. Let me know if anything comes up."

"Will do. And, Ben, be careful out there. Ranches can be like islands. You're out in the middle of nowhere with no one to depend on but yourselves."

"I know that. And the local authorities aren't helping at all."

Ben hung up and burst through the door as a horse and its rider galloped across the dry grasses toward the house.

"That's Eddy." Mrs. Henderson stood on the porch, wiping her hands on a dry dish towel. "He's in an all-fired hurry."

Kate was halfway to the fence, with Cara Jo following, when Ben leaped off the porch.

Eddy's mount galloped across the dry Texas paddock of sparse grass and scraggly vegetation. By the time he reached the gate, Kate was holding it open for him.

Ben ground to a halt beside her. "What's wrong?" Ben asked.

Eddy slipped from the saddle, his boots hitting the ground, stirring up a puff of dust. "Found several steer carcasses along the southern boundary."

Chapter Ten

"I didn't know if you wanted to come out and inspect, or if you wanted me to notify the sheriff's department and let them handle it." Eddy waited for Kate's response.

Kate glanced at Ben. "I don't think the sheriff will be much help. Let's get out there and see what we've got." Kate headed for the barn. "Oh, wait.... Lily." Kate performed an about-face and headed back to the house.

Just inside the kitchen door, Lily held Pickles to her cheek as she stood beside Cara Jo.

"Kate, go on, do what you have to do." Cara Jo waved Kate toward the barn. "Don't worry about Miss Lily. She and I are going to start training Pickles. Aren't we, dear?"

Lily nodded. "Mrs. Henderson's making treats for Pickles."

Kate bit down on her lip. "Are you sure?"

Cara Jo smiled. "Absolutely."

"Don't you have to be at the diner?"

"Not today. I give myself a day off every once in a while. I can do that." She smiled. "I'm the owner."

"Thanks." Kate spun and hurried to the barn where Eddy and Ben stood.

Her first time in the barn, Kate stared around at the tack hanging from hooks on the walls. "Is there a four-wheeler or a horse I can ride?"

Eddy shook his head. "No four-wheelers, but I've got a couple horses in the stalls in the barn."

Ben captured her arms and turned her to face him. "You're not going. You need to stay and look after Lily."

"You saw what Marge is capable of." Kate nodded toward Eddy. "She wields a powerful shotgun, doesn't she?"

Eddy slapped his hat against his thigh. "Scares me, if that's whatcha mean." He slipped a rifle into the holster on his saddle.

Kate felt a little better knowing they'd be heading out with a little more firepower than her Glock, which was tucked neatly into Ben's waistband, along with the one he wore on a shoulder holster over his blue chambray shirt. She made up her mind. "Lily will be fine with Mrs. H. and Cara Jo will be there as well to entertain her and keep an eye out for trouble."

Ben crossed his arms. "Sounds like you thought this through."

"I did."

"I still don't think it's a good idea."

Her brows rose. "Why not? This is my ranch, and it's my responsibility to see to the safety of the people and animals on it." She stepped toward one of the occupied stalls. "I'm going."

Ben followed, his boots stirring the dust around her. "Have you ever ridden a horse?"

"Plenty," she lied. Well, it wasn't a lie if "plenty" meant five times in her entire life.

"Right." Ben's one-word response told Kate he didn't believe her for a minute.

Eddy led a horse from the middle stall. "This is Lucky. She's a little older and as calm a horse as we have on the Flying K."

"As compared to what?" Kate asked as she stared up at the horse, thinking the mare was bigger than any of the horses she'd ever ridden.

"She's been out roaming the pastures since Mr. K....left." Eddy breathed deeply, his jaw tightening. "She won't be hard to ride."

Kate refused to be intimidated by the animal's size. "You'll have to show me where everything is."

Eddy led the way to the racks of saddles stored in the tack room. He nodded toward a brightly colored blanket. "If you'll toss that over Lucky's back, I'll handle the saddle."

Rather than push the point and take the saddle herself, Kate led the way back out to the horse and eased the blanket across Lucky's back.

The animal eased sideways, whickering softly.

Kate stepped away and let Eddy settle the saddle on the horse's back. She studied Eddy's moves, committing them to memory for the next time when she'd insist on doing it herself.

"When you cinch the girth on Lucky, do it a couple of times. She likes to blow her belly out. If you don't do it more than once, she'll fool you and when you get going, the saddle will slide to the side, dumping the rider."

Kate nodded. "I'll remember."

Once Eddy had the saddle securely fastened, he handed the bridle to Kate. "You can do this."

Kate nodded, trying to remember, from the five times she'd ridden at a farm outside Houston, how to slip the bridle between the horse's teeth and over its head.

Eddy walked away, calling over his shoulder, "She'll bite down to keep you from getting it between her teeth. Stick your thumb in the corner of her mouth to get her to open."

While Eddy adjusted the girth on his horse, Kate worked at sliding the bridle between Lucky's teeth. After several failed attempts, the horse stomped her feet and swished her tail, slapping Kate at like a pesky fly.

"You're going to wear this bridle," Kate said between gritted teeth.

In her peripheral vision, Kate could see Ben walking toward her. She'd be damned if she couldn't accomplish this one little task. With her teeth clenched as tightly as Lucky's, and the bridle held in one hand, Kate shoved her thumb in the corner of the animal's mouth and tugged.

Lucky smacked her lips and her teeth opened wide enough for Kate to slide the bridle between her teeth and loop the strap over her ears. "There. That wasn't so bad, was it?"

The mare opened and closed her mouth as if adjusting to the metal bit.

Kate tightened the strap beneath Lucky's chin and the one around her head. When Lucky was ready, Kate walked her to the barn door and glanced at the stirrup, wondering how in hell she was going to get her foot up that high. She glanced around the barnyard, spying a wooden step close to a hitching post. She tugged the reins, urging the horse to follow.

Lucky straightened her legs, refusing to move.

Ben had saddled a gray Arabian gelding and stood in the barnyard watching Kate struggle with the mare. "Need a hand?"

"No, I have this," she insisted.

"Lucky doesn't like the step." Eddy led his gelding out and swung up into the saddle.

Ben closed the distance between Kate and himself.

An uncontrollable surge of excitement swept over her, setting Kate's nerve endings alight.

"Let me help," he whispered. "It by no means implies you need it." Ben stooped, cupping his hands.

Kate leaned close. "I don't like relying on you." She stepped into his palms.

"Why?" He rose, lifting her high enough to toss her leg over the saddle.

"Because you won't always be there. I'll have to take care of myself and Lily." She held on to the saddle horn with one hand.

Ben nudged her calf.

His fingers touching her, even through the thick denim of her jeans, had her blood racing through her veins. She held her leg well out of his way while he adjusted the stirrup on the right and rounded the horse to adjust the left. When he had it positioned correctly, he guided her foot into the stirrup. Then he handed Kate the reins and stepped back.

Lucky danced to the side, setting loose a swarm of butterflies in Kate's belly. Now was the time to admit she hadn't ridden a horse in over ten years. But she clamped down hard on her bottom lip and held on for dear life.

Ben swung up in his saddle, turning the gelding all in one smooth motion, like he'd done this a thousand times before.

Since he'd grown up on a ranch, he probably had.

Her back ramrod-straight, Kate nudged Lucky with her heels and followed Eddy to the gate.

Ben covered the rear.

Eddy leaned down and pulled the lever, opening the gate.

Lucky bolted through and set off at a gallop.

Her heart in her throat, Kate pulled back on the reins, wishing she hadn't been so quick to say she'd ride out. No matter how hard she tugged on the leather straps, her efforts only slowed the mare marginally.

Ben and Eddy caught up to her before she'd gone far.

The ranch foreman passed her and led the way to the southwest corner of the ranch.

Ben and his gelding kept pace beside her.

"This is the first time you've been out to see what you now own?"

She nodded. The thought of all that she could see around her belonging to her seemed a bit overwhelming. "What do I do with all this?"

"That's why you hire people like Eddy to take care of the horses, cattle and whatever else you decide to raise."

"I've never been one to sit back and watch others do all

the work. It bothers me to have Mrs. Henderson cooking meals and cleaning up after me. I've never had anyone wait on me. Not even my own mother." Kate stared at Eddy's back, wondering what it meant to be a working rancher and if she had what it took to do it.

"Ranching is hard work."

Kate sat up straight, though her tailbone was beginning to hurt. "I'm not afraid of hard work."

"It's twenty-four hours a day, three hundred and sixty-five days a year."

She smiled. "So is parenting."

"Lily needs a mother to take care of her."

"And I need to make this place operate at a rate that can support us. Otherwise, I'll have to find a job to support *it*. And out here in South Texas, I doubt there are jobs that pay enough to support a woman and her child, much less her ranch."

Ben touched the brim of his hat. "You have a point. Owning a ranch is a big responsibility. Are you sure you want to bite off that much?"

Kate frowned at him. "Now you're sounding like Deputy Schillinger. I'm not a quitter."

"What about the danger?"

"I'm not a quitter," she repeated, staring ahead at Eddy.

"What about Lily?"

Kate bit down on her bottom lip. That was the rub. Had it just been Kate, she'd have jumped in with both feet ready to rip into anyone stupid enough to try to run her off her land. Now she had a child to protect. And she had to give Lily a home.

Funny how, after only two days, she'd started thinking of the Flying K as home. Her home. Though she still didn't know much about the man who'd lived here, the man who'd been a big factor in bringing her into this world, she felt a tenuous connection to him and wished not once but a hundred times that she'd had the opportunity to know the man. "Lily needs a place to call home."

"Isn't home where the heart is? Wouldn't she be happy anywhere as long as she's with you?"

Anger bubbled up in her chest. "Are you trying to talk me into leaving?"

"No, I'm trying to figure out why you want to stay when all you've gotten out of it so far is threats and attacks."

As quickly as it rose, the anger ebbed away. "I've also made a new friend." She smiled. "And I met you." She glanced at him, her brows rising.

Ben's gaze remained forward as if he avoided hers. "That's not much of a bonus."

"I think so." She gave him a moment of silence before asking, "I understand we're a painful reminder of your family. But is it that bad that you still want to leave us?"

"Damn it, yes." His response startled the horse beneath him.

The gelding sidestepped, bumping into Kate's.

Ben's leg brushed against Kate's calf. He jerked the reins to the left and the horse danced away. But the brief contact had been enough to leave Kate's breath ragged, her hands shaking.

For a few long moments, Kate rode in silence, her heart hammering against her ribs. Ben wasn't afraid of evil men with guns. He feared her and Lily. It all made sense.

He'd lost his wife and daughter. Seeing Kate and Lily had to be tearing him apart. Kate's heart tightened as if someone had hold of it, squeezing mightily. She'd lost a husband she'd loved with all her heart. Kate couldn't imagine losing her spouse and her daughter all at once. She doubted she'd be strong enough to go on living.

Ben was afraid to care again.

Eddy shouted and kicked his horse in the flanks. Black

buzzards rose from the ground ahead, their huge wingspan filling the air, stirring dust into a cloud.

Relieved to have something else to concentrate on, Kate eased her horse forward, bringing the mare to a halt beside Eddy.

The stench of decaying flesh almost knocked her out of the saddle. Kate gasped and sucked in another lungful of the putrid air. She pulled her shirt up over her nose and breathed through the fabric.

Spread across the ground was the carcass of a black Angus steer, mostly picked over by the scavenger birds who'd located this meal.

Eddy and Ben dropped out of their saddles and squatted beside the dead animal.

"Whoever killed it used a knife." Ben pointed to the smooth edges of cut skin on what once had been the steer's throat.

Kate gagged and swallowed hard to keep from vomiting. She sucked in a deep breath through her shirt and let go of it. Then she grabbed the saddle horn, slipped her feet from the stirrup and slid down the horse's side, landing with a thump on her butt.

Ben was beside her, grasping her beneath her arms. "You all right?"

"I'm fine, except for my damaged pride." She stood and brushed the dirt from her hands and backside. "Who would have done this?"

"Considering they cut away the biggest chunks of meat, I'd say someone who was looking for a meal. *Madre de Dios.*" Eddy rattled off a couple sentences in Spanish before he shook his head and stood.

Ben was circling the dead animal. "There are footprints all around." After a moment he looked off into the brush to the south. "They lead toward the canyon."

"Shouldn't we follow them?"

Ben shook his head. "Only if you want to die."

A shiver rocked Kate's frame. "You think the people who killed this cow would shoot at us?"

"No, but they might slit your throat to keep you from disclosing their location."

"Oh." Kate wrapped her arms around her middle, the warmth of the day turning cool. "What now?"

Eddy looked out over the land. "We need to herd all the strays closer to the ranch house and barn where we can keep a closer watch on them."

"Doesn't that limit the amount of grazing?" Kate cast a glance at the dry land, where vegetation was sparse.

"Do you have a better suggestion?" Ben asked.

Kate stared across at Ben and Eddy. "We could call in the Customs and Border Protection and have them run interference until they get the drug trafficking under control."

"We'll report it," Ben said. "But getting the illegal activity under control won't happen overnight." He gathered his reins and led the gelding away from the dead steer. "In the meantime, we need to do like Eddy said. Otherwise you'll continue to lose cattle."

Eddy glanced at the sun tipping toward the horizon. "We can start tomorrow. It's getting late and we shouldn't be out here after dark."

Kate walked her mare a few steps away from the carnage and reached high for the saddle horn, dragging herself up enough to get her foot in the stirrup. At last she was able to sling her leg over the saddle. Proud she'd gotten up by herself, she almost cried when she noticed the reins hanging from the bit down to the ground.

A soft chuckle sounded beside her.

Ben walked across the dry ground, bent to retrieve the reins and handed them up to her without a word. That quirky smile almost made her want to kick him. At the same time it made her insides heat with want. She pushed aside her desire and focused on the next step.

The three of them rode back the way they'd come, with Eddy taking the lead again.

Halfway back to the barn, Ben shouted to Eddy, "Go on ahead. Kate and I are going to do a little target practice."

Eddy chuckled. "Can you wait until I get out of range? I prefer to remain in one piece."

"You bet." Ben reined in beside Kate and dropped to the ground. He grasped her around the waist and lifted her out of the saddle.

When she opened her mouth to protest, he covered her lips with a finger. "I know you can get down all by yourself. Just humor me. It'll be faster and you won't need to spend any more time with me than you have to."

She rested her hands on his shoulders as he let her slowly slide down the front of his body until her feet touched down. Kate clamped hard on her tongue, afraid she'd say what she really thought. That his hands on her waist had been deliciously sexy, the broad fingers spanning her middle, his muscles flexing and the ease with which he'd lifted her had left her breathless. But not nearly as air-deprived as the feel of his body against hers as she'd slid down him to her feet.

She'd do best to keep her mouth shut and get this lesson over with. The more time she spent alone with Ben, the more she couldn't imagine him leaving. Dangerous ground to be sure.

BEN REGRETTED LIFTING her from the saddle as soon as his hands closed around her. He compounded the regret by letting her body brush against his. Now all he wanted was to do it again, only this time for her to wrap her legs around his waist, her breasts pressing against his chest.

He pulled the Glock from his back waistband and checked the safety.

Kate stood with her back to him. She'd pulled the rubber band from her hair, letting it fall free around her shoulders. After she'd finger-combed it several times she gathered the long tresses in a bunch.

Ben shoved the pistol into his pocket and pushed Kate's hands aside, plucking the band from her fingers. In two quick motions he had the ponytail secured. His hands dropped to her arms, turning her to face him.

She blinked up at him, her lips parted, full and kissable. "You do that like a natural."

"Comes from having a daughter, much like Lily." His hands fell to his sides and he turned away.

He strode several feet away from Kate, needing the distance to keep from pawing her like a teenager. His member strained against the tight confines of his denim jeans. God, he wanted the woman. Instead, he scanned the terrain, searching for a target.

"Kate," he called out.

She came to him, her hands twisting together, her brows just as knotted. "We can do this another day," she said.

"No, you need to know how to use that gun if you plan to keep it."

"Okay." Kate nodded. "Show me."

He handed her the Glock and wrapped her fingers around the grip, lacing one finger over the trigger.

Her body shook against him.

"Think of it as an extension of your arms." He helped her cup her trigger hand with the palm of her empty hand and raised her arms.

"Look down the barrel and line up the sight with the target."

"What am I aiming for?" she asked, holding the gun steady.

"See the prickly pear cactus there with the three lobes facing us?"

"Yes."

"Aim at the top center lobe. Once you have the sights lined up, press the trigger slowly."

Her pulse hammered through her veins. "Will it kick?"

"Not much."

"How much is not much?" she asked.

"Just shoot it and you'll find out."

She aimed the barrel toward the cactus, breathed in, then out, then closed her eyes and pulled the trigger.

The pop wasn't as loud as she'd expected and the kick wasn't bad at all. She focused on the cactus, noticing all three lobes remained intact. "Did I miss?"

"Yes, and you scared the crap out of me." He pushed his cowboy hat back on his head and circled behind her, his arms coming up on either side. "Let's do it again. Only this time, keep your eyes open."

Ben spooned her body with his, bringing his arms up on either side of hers. His hands closed around her fingers and he inhaled her unique scent of honeysuckle and citrus.

His groin tightened and he knew he was in trouble.

Chapter Eleven

Ben's breath stirred the tendrils of hair hanging loose from her ponytail. Kate leaned her back against the solid wall of muscles that was her bodyguard cowboy. The warmth of his arms around her reassured and scared her all at once.

What would it be like to lie in his arms naked?

Her hands shook so badly, she thought she might drop the gun.

"Are you afraid?" he whispered.

Yes, yes, she was afraid. Afraid of falling in love with a stranger. Afraid of investing her emotions in someone who would leave as soon as the threat was neutralized. Afraid she and Lily would be heartbroken when the dust settled on the Flying K Ranch. "N-no," she lied, "I'm not afraid."

"Good. This time keep your eyes open and caress the trigger like a lover."

Holy shotgun blasts! Was he kidding her? All his words did was make her even more aware of the ridge of his fly pressing into her buttocks. She wanted to caress something, and it wasn't the trigger of her 9 mm Glock.

Perspiration beaded on her forehead. "Is it getting hotter?"

"You bet." His hand curved around her again. "Ready?"

Oh, hell, yes, but not for what he was thinking.

Focus, woman. Hell, how could she when she had the hottest cowboy in Texas wrapped around her?

Think of Lily. Images of her daughter brought Kate back to the real reason for her shooting lessons. Living alone on a ranch, she had to have the ability to protect herself and her daughter.

Her hand tightened around the grip and she forced air into and out of her lungs, focusing her concentration down the short barrel, lining up the sights with the target. Then, like Ben said, she stroked the trigger, keeping her eyes wide open.

The weapon kicked backward and Kate almost dropped it.

The acrid scent of burned gunpowder filled her nostrils and she blinked to clear her vision.

"I'll be damned." Ben leaned to her side and stared at her, his brows furrowed. "Are you sure you haven't done this before?"

"No." Dear God, his face was close enough to kiss. So much for maintaining focus on the lesson. "Why?" Her voice cracked and her body trembled.

"Take a look." He faced what was left of the cactus. The top, middle lobe had a hole blasted through it.

Kate squinted, afraid she was seeing things. Sure enough, there was a smooth round hole, dead center. A thrill of excitement rippled through her. "I did that?"

"You did." He chuckled. "I think you've taken me for a ride. How many times have you handled this gun?"

Kate shook her head, floored by her accuracy. "Other than using it to hit the intruder over the head the other night, never."

"I believe you have a promising career ahead of you as a sharpshooter or sniper."

"It was luck." Kate laughed shakily.

He nodded toward the cactus. "Do it again, only this time, aim for the right lobe." His hands fell to his sides and he backed away.

Standing alone, she didn't feel as confident or steady. But

she also wasn't distracted by body contact. She looked down the barrel and lined up the right lobe in her sights.

"Remember…caress the trigger." Ben's words slid over her like melted chocolate in the dry Texas heat. Her hand tightened around the grip and the trigger and the weapon discharged.

Kate yelped. "Dang. I wasn't ready." She glanced at the cactus. "Did I hit anything?"

Ben chuckled. "The dirt in front of the plant."

Widening her stance, Kate glared at Ben. "I'm going to get this."

He nodded. "I have no doubt."

"Shh." This time her hands didn't quiver, her body didn't budge and the bullet nicked the lower corner of the lobe she'd aimed at. Her gaze shot to Ben. "Does that count?"

"If it had been a man, you most likely would have hit him where it would hurt him." Ben grinned. "That's good."

Kate couldn't look away. When Ben smiled, his entire face lit up and his blue eyes shone bright and clear. She tipped her head to the side. "I like it when you smile."

Immediately, his mouth straightened and he glanced away. "Adjust how you line up the sight based on where it hit last time, and keep practicing." Ben strode to where they'd tied the horses.

Kate took her time and fired again. The bullet bit into the top corner of the cactus lobe. Her concentration alternated between the target and Ben. He'd gone from happy to glum in seconds and it was driving her nuts.

"You know, it wouldn't kill you to smile more often." She cast a glance over her shoulder at the silent man.

He flipped the stirrup over the saddle on his horse and he tightened the girth before he muttered, "Have to have something to smile about."

"I heard that." Kate lined up the sights and squeezed off another round. The bullet pierced the center of the right lobe.

Kate smiled and looked back at Ben, careful to point the nose of the pistol away from him. "How about waking up every day?"

"What about it?"

"Aren't you happy when you wake up every day?" Kate continued. "How can you be unhappy when the sun is shining?"

"The sunshine makes it incredibly hot out here in South Texas."

Kate fired off the remaining rounds in her ten-round magazine. Some of the shots went where they were supposed to, others hit the dirt in front of and behind the cactus plant, never touching it. When the last bullet was spent, she hit the magazine release button and caught the magazine before it hit the ground. The sun dipped low on the horizon, lengthening Kate's shadow.

She crossed to where Ben stood holding his horse's reins and stared up into his eyes.

The shadows were back and his jaw was tight, a muscle twitching in his left cheek.

Before she could overthink her reaction to his somber look, Kate smoothed her hand over the twitching muscle. "You must have loved her a lot."

Ben grabbed her wrist so fast, Kate cried out. "I loved Julia and I loved Sarah," he said, taking her gun in his other hand and tucking it back into his waistband. "But nothing I do now will bring them back. Nothing. They're gone."

His fingers hurt where he crushed her wrist, but Kate couldn't pull it free, nor could she back away from the intensity of his gaze.

"Julia and Sarah died, Ben." She pressed a hand to his chest. "But they never left you."

Silence settled like dust between them.

For a long moment, nothing stirred, neither one of them moved.

Then Ben yanked her hard against his chest, his lips crashing down over hers, his mouth claiming hers in a savage kiss. He let go of her wrist, one hand cupping the back of her head, the other clutching her bottom, grinding her pelvis against the hard ridge beneath his fly.

When he let her come up for air, his lips moved over hers, sliding along her chin. "I loved my wife."

"Yes, you did. But you didn't die with her."

"I know, damn it." He grabbed her arms and shook her. "I should have."

"No, Ben. You're still here for a reason."

His head whipped up. "What for? To punish me for failing to protect them?" He shoved her away from him. "I wasn't there for them."

"You didn't kill them."

"I could have stopped him."

"You couldn't be everywhere. He'd have found a way."

Ben stalked away, breathing hard, his face a ruddy red.

Kate's heart squeezed so hard in her chest, she thought she might have a heart attack. The anguish in Ben's face, the agony in his tone, ripped her apart.

"We need to go. It's getting dark."

When Ben passed her to get to his horse, Kate touched his arm.

He shook off her hand. "Don't." His glare scorched her.

Kate flinched, drawing back her hand as if he'd burned it. "I'm sorry. I shouldn't have brought it up."

He snorted and swung up into the saddle without offering her a leg up.

Kate managed to mount on her own, struggling to keep Ben's anger and withdrawal from bringing her all the way down. The man had some issues.

Hell, so did she. Only she'd had four years to work through them. Two years and a wake-up call in the form of Kate and Lily hadn't been enough time to lessen Ben's loss. He was still mourning his wife and child and nothing Kate could do or say would mend that kind of broken heart.

As Kate turned her mare north toward the house, a light blinked from the south. A shot of adrenaline raced through her system and she tugged hard on Lucky's reins, wheeling her around to face south again.

"Did you see that?" Kate glanced over her shoulder at Ben.

Lucky jerked her head and whinnied, trying to get Kate to turn back toward the barn.

Ben was already a few yards north when he reined in and twisted in his saddle. "See what?"

"A light." Kate pointed. "Out there."

Ben urged his horse around and came to a halt beside Kate. "Where?"

As dusk settled in around Kate, her eyes adjusted to the darkness. A flash of light blinked on, then off, a tiny pinprick on the horizon. "There." She gathered her reins. "Should we go check it out?"

Ben studied the light. "No."

"But—" The light grew more steady, pointed directly at them.

"No, looks like they're headed this way and we don't have time to outrun them." He spun his horse and dug in his heels. "Come on."

Kate stared at the light a fraction of a second longer. It was getting bigger. Which meant Ben was right, the vehicle causing the light was headed their way. Whether it was friend or foe, Kate had no intention of sticking around to find out.

She swung Lucky around and took off after Ben and his gelding, letting Lucky have her head.

Ben raced across the ground, dodging cactus, sage and saw palmetto. When he came to a dry ravine, he reined in so fast, Kate's horse struggled to stop in time. Tire tracks led down the banks and back up the other side.

Ben was off his horse and reaching for her reins before Kate had time to think. "Why did we stop?"

"We won't make it back to the safety of the ranch before they catch up. We have to find a place to hide." He reached up, grabbed her around the waist and pulled her off the horse. "Hurry."

Ben took the reins of both the horses and ran down the banks, following the meandering creek bed.

Kate hurried after him, slipping and sliding on the loose gravel and rocks. "Do you think whoever is out there is dangerous?"

"You want to stick around and find out?" he said over his shoulder.

Kate closed her mouth, conserving her energy to keep up with Ben's headlong race down the wash.

When he came to a point where the creek bed curved north at a huge boulder, he tugged the horses behind the outcropping and tied their reins to a scrubby root. They were a good two hundred yards from the tracks. "Stay here."

Kate skidded to a halt, breathing hard. "Why? Where are you going?"

"Back to see who's trespassing." He turned and started back the way they'd come.

Kate laid a hand on his arm. "Not without me, you're not."

"It'll be dangerous."

"It's my land. I need to see what's going on." She let her hand slip down to his.

"It's safer staying clear." The darkness was settling in around them and the stars popped out of the sky one at a time.

Kate couldn't read the expression in Ben's eyes, but she wouldn't let him go without her. She dropped his hand and crossed her arms. "If you don't take me with you, I'll follow you anyway."

Ben sucked in a deep breath and let it out. "You're a stubborn woman."

"I've been known to be. Are you going to stand around arguing or are we going to go and find a good place to hide closer to the road?"

"I don't like it."

She snorted. "So noted."

"Then stay behind me and keep quiet."

"Yes, sir." Kate popped a salute that was all but lost on him as he turned and jogged back down the creek bed, hunkering low so that he wouldn't be seen over the banks.

Kate followed, copying his technique, her heart pounding, her breathing erratic. What was she getting herself into?

All she knew was that she didn't want to be left behind while Ben risked his life to see what was going down on her ranch.

Light glinted above them, casting a beam over the top of their heads.

Ben came to a sudden stop and flung his arm out, catching her before she barreled past him. "We hide here."

He ducked behind a boulder no bigger than a sheep and dragged her down beside him. Ben pulled the Glock from the back of his jeans and handed it to Kate. "Don't use this unless I tell you to." He removed his 9 mm from his shoulder holster and held it in front of his face.

Kate's hand trembled. Sure she'd been practicing shooting, but the thought of pulling the trigger on a person...

Her shoulders stiffened, her resolve strengthening as she thought of Lily. She'd do whatever it took to protect the ones she loved.

The rumble of an engine grew louder and the light brighter. Then it angled down the creek bank and came to a grinding halt, dust flying all around, forming a hazy glow in front of the truck. The driver turned the vehicle off and silence engulfed the scene.

As the dust settled, Kate peered at the back of the pickup.

Four men perched on the sides, wielding what looked like automatic weapons, the type used by the military.

Kate gasped, then clamped a hand over her mouth and stared wide-eyed as one man hopped out, his feet crunching as he landed in the gravel. He stretched, his gun arm rising high into the night sky. He said something in Spanish and the driver responded.

Another man, brandishing a similar weapon, dropped down and shone a flashlight in a wide beam around the pickup, turning it slowly toward the position where Kate and Ben lay.

Ben whispered, "Close your eyes."

Kate squeezed them shut and ducked her head low behind the boulder.

The crunch of gravel grew louder. Kate fought her instinct to look up and see how close the men had come, but she was afraid that if she looked, the flashlight would glint off her eyes and give away their position.

"Brille la luz aquí!" a voice shouted closer than Kate had imagined.

Ben pressed his lips to her ear. "Don't move," he whispered.

He didn't have to worry. She froze, holding her breath, waiting for the men to move away.

Light shone on either side of the boulder.

Then a loud bang blasted through the night and kicked up dust around where Kate hovered. She bit hard on her tongue to keep from crying out.

Footsteps crunched closer and then a heavily accented voice called out. *"Serpiente para cenar!"*

Men laughed and the light bobbed skyward.

The footsteps moved away.

Kate let go of the breath she'd been holding and dared to peer around the side of the boulder.

One man had his gun slung over his shoulder and he held

a long fat snake out to the side, speaking in rapid Spanish. The driver and the other gunmen laughed.

The crackle of a radio broke through their merriment and the driver responded to the call. When he finished, he waved a hand out the window. *"Vayamos!"*

The snake man dropped the reptile and leaped over the side of the pickup. The other men leaped in beside him. The truck pulled up the other side of the wash as another set of lights crested the bank behind them and dipped down into the creek.

In that one instant the light from the second vehicle illuminated the truck in front of it. Kate could see into the first truck's bed.

Huddled low and holding on to one another were several women and young girls.

One cried out.

One of the gunmen slapped the girl. *"Silencio!"*

Kate lurched forward, her heart lodged in her throat.

Ben captured her arm and dragged her back to the ground. "Don't move." He pushed her back to the ground and started to get up himself.

This time she caught his arm and held on to Ben. "There's too many of them."

"Alto!" The gunman with the flashlight shone the beam over the creek bed for a long moment, the light hovering over the top of the small boulder.

Kate ground her teeth and fought her instinct to leap out and scratch the man's eyes out who'd slapped the girl. But even she knew it would be crazy. They outnumbered Kate and Ben and outgunned their two pistols. Taking a stand would be suicide.

After a moment, the gunman waved the driver on and the truck topped the incline and pulled away. The second truck lumbered down into the ravine and up the other side, revealing the back filled with four more gunmen and from the dark forms hunkered low in the bed, another load of people.

Ben lay still for a long time, even after the second truck exited the creek and moved off across the desert.

"Why didn't we stop them?"

"My duty is to protect you. We were outnumbered. The best we can do is get back to the ranch and report this to the Customs and Border Protection."

"But those women and the girls…" Kate stood and brushed the dust off her jeans.

"Coyotes would just as soon kill them, ditch them and save their own butts." Ben headed back down the creek bed toward where they'd stashed the horses.

Kate was left to follow, wishing with all her heart she could have done more to protect the frightened people in the back of the trucks.

Ben untied the horses, bent to give her a boost up and swung up into his saddle without speaking another word.

They hurried across the dried grasses, dodging cacti and stumpy palmetto palms illuminated by the sparkling blanket of stars in the sky.

"Do you think they could be the people responsible for killing the steer?" Kate called out over the thrumming of horses' hooves.

"Probably."

"We should have stopped them."

Ben shot a glance her way. The moon had begun to rise, reflecting light off Ben's eyes. "The only way we'd go back out there at night is with a full contingent of soldiers and the Customs and Border Protection agents leading the way. Even then, *you're* not going out there."

A chill gave her gooseflesh as she recalled the guns every one of the men carried.

Ben urged his horse into a gallop, cutting off any further conversation.

Kate dug her heels into her horse's flanks, her gaze panning the horizon, searching for the lights of the two vehicles. Her breathing returned to normal only after the glowing windows of the ranch house came into view.

They rode up to the gate at full gallop.

Eddy stood ready, swinging the gate open for them. "You two are in a hurry. Run into trouble?"

"Two trucks full of gunmen and people." Ben dropped down off his gelding. "We had to lay low until they passed."

"You did right getting back here." Eddy nodded toward his horse. "I was getting worried and was about to come out searching for you."

Kate led her horse into the barn. Before Ben or Eddy could offer to help, she'd flipped her stirrup up over the saddle and loosened the girth. Not so hard. She could get used to riding the range and checking on cattle.

When it came time to haul the saddle off the horse, Kate tugged, expecting it to be difficult. But she pulled too hard and the saddle slid right off, the weight sending her flying back.

Ben's arms circled her waist, steadying her.

Kate leaned into him for a moment, appreciating the solid muscles and the earthy scent of a man who'd been working with horses. She could get used to having him around.

Kate pushed away. "We need to get up to the house and call the CBP." She ducked around Ben and hurried to deposit the saddle in the tack room before she did something stupid…again.

Brush in hand, Eddy stood beside Kate's mare. "I'll take care of the horses. You two head on up to the house."

"Thanks." Ben hooked Kate's arm and led her out of the barn and up to the house.

She was kind of glad to have him so close. After hiding from gunmen, the night's shadows caused her a lot more heebie-jeebies than ever before. Before she'd seen the two truckloads of coyotes and women, Kate had been more than ready to call this place home and make a stand for the land her father left for her and Lily. But now...

Kate and Ben only made it halfway across the yard when Lily burst through the screen door and raced down the steps. "Mommy!"

Ben let Kate's arm drop. "I'll make the call."

"Thanks." Kate gathered Lily up in a bear hug and swung her around. "How's my sweetie pie?" She held the child longer than normal and inhaled the scent of baby shampoo. An image of the women and girls in the backs of those trucks had been indelibly etched in her memory. She couldn't imagine being so desperate she'd subject Lily to the danger of stealing across the border in the middle of the night with men who'd just as soon take the money and leave them for dead.

"We made cookies. I found a horny toad, but it got away. Pickles piddled in the hall twice and he's asleep now." Lily glanced over Kate's shoulder at the barn. "Can I ride a horse?"

"Not now, baby."

"When?"

"Another day." A day when Kate felt more comfortable about the horse she'd be riding, and after they found the gunmen traversing her land and jailed them where they couldn't traffic humans or drugs ever again. Maybe then she could be more certain about making the Flying K their home forever.

"Come see our cookies." Lily wiggled out of Kate's arms and ran for the house.

Kate followed Ben and Lily into the house.

Once inside, Ben headed for the hallway.

Kate entered the kitchen where Lily showed her the cookies she'd made with Mrs. Henderson and Cara Jo.

Cara Jo was stacking cooled cookies in the cookie jar. "I'm so glad you two made it back when you did. I was about to call the sheriff."

"I'll tell you about it after Lily is in bed." Kate glanced around. "Where's Mrs. Henderson?"

"Her husband picked her up an hour ago."

"Thanks for staying with Lily. I owe you."

"I enjoyed it as much as I think she did."

"Now, let me see if these cookies are edible." Kate grabbed a cookie from the pile and bit into it, her empty stomach rumbling. "Oh, yes. They are wonderful. Snicker-doodles?" she asked.

Lily laughed. "How did you know?"

"My mother used to make these." Tears welled in her eyes at the memory of her mother and the weekends they'd spent making cookies and hanging out when she was little like Lily. At times like this, she missed her so much it hurt.

Kate glanced at the clock. "Holy smokes, it's way past your bedtime, young lady."

"I already had my bath. Miss Cara Jo let me stay up until you got home so that I could show you the cookies."

Cara Jo winced. "I hope you don't mind. She was so excited."

Kate shook her head. "Not at all. But now it's time for bed."

Lily danced ahead of Kate. "Can Miss Cara Jo read a book to me?"

"I'm sure she would like to get home sometime tonight and it's a long way back to town."

Lily grabbed one of Kate's hands and one of Cara Jo's and looked up at them both with her wide green eyes. "Please?"

Cara Jo laughed. "I'd love to and it'll give you a chance to wash up and have dinner."

"You're sure?"

"Absolutely." She swung Lily's arm. "Lily and I are best buds, aren't we? Why don't you grab Pickles and let's get her settled in her box upstairs."

Lily chased Pickles down the hallway and up the stairs.

Kate hugged her new friend. "Thanks, Cara Jo."

"Really, Kate. I love Lily, she's a great kid." Cara Jo climbed the stairs behind Lily, leaving Kate at the bottom.

Ben slipped up beside her. "I made the call. They're sending out a chopper to see if they can locate the trucks."

Kate faced him, her heartbeat speeding up at his proximity. Why did this man she'd only known a very short time have that kind of pull on her? "Any chance they'll find them?"

"The trucks have a big head start in the amount of time it took us to ride back to the ranch." He shrugged. "They could be just about anywhere by now."

Kate rested her hand on the banister and stared up the stairs, her heart heavy. "Do you think they're helping illegal immigrants or trafficking women?" Kate gazed into Ben's eyes.

His brows dipped low and a muscle jerked in his jaw. "As far as I could see, there were only women and girls in those trucks."

"Dear lord." Kate sagged and her stomach roiled. "We should have stopped them."

"No. We were outnumbered and not as heavily armed." Ben gripped her arms and turned her toward him. "Let the Border Patrol deal with it. They have the resources and the weapons necessary to handle the coyotes. Had we intervened, we would only have made matters worse."

"Still…"

"Have faith in the CBP."

"Do you?"

Ben's lips tightened. "At this point, I have to. I have to focus on you. I can't risk your life chasing after bad guys." He turned and would have walked away, but Kate put a hand on his arm.

"Ben, what happened out there?"

"What do you mean?"

"Between us." She stopped, her gaze dropping to where her hand touched his arm. "Before the coyotes… The kiss."

He stiffened, drawing up to his full height. "What happened out there…shouldn't have. I won't let it happen again."

Kate braced her palms on his chest. The solid muscles beneath his shirt made her long to run her fingers across his naked skin. "I shouldn't have encouraged it. But…"

"It won't happen again. I'm here to protect you and Lily. Nothing more." He backed away, his tone brooking no more argument, his face set in stone.

Kate tucked her hands in her pockets to keep them from shaking. She wanted to say more, to tell him she'd felt his response, he wasn't immune to her. Instead, she turned and walked up the stairs.

IT TOOK ALL of Ben's self-control to keep from going up the stairs after Kate. He wanted her so badly it hurt and the turmoil it was causing inside him was more than he could stand.

Kate was as different from Julia as night from day. She'd already proved she wasn't afraid of anything. When the gunmen had shot so close to them, Kate hadn't fallen apart like a lot of women would have. She'd held steady and stayed low.

He wondered what Julia would have done. What she had done when she and his daughter had been…

Ben's breath lodged in his throat when he realized he couldn't even remember Julia's face. He closed his eyes, but all he could see was light auburn hair, glinting like copper in the sun.

Ben stepped out onto the porch.

Eddy was coming up from the barn. "I have the horses settled in for the night and gave them an extra section of hay."

"Thanks."

Eddy climbed the steps and stood beside Ben, staring out into the night as he rocked back on his boot heels. "Well, I'll be heading home unless you think I need to stay."

"No. Go on home. I'll take it from here."

"Think she'll stay?"

Ben didn't have to ask who Eddy was talking about. "Kate's a pretty determined woman."

Eddy nodded. "If she's anything like her father, she won't give up easily."

No, she wouldn't, but in this case, maybe she should. The situation was too dangerous.

"I'll be goin'. *Buenas noches.*" Eddy climbed into his pickup and drove away, leaving behind him a deep silence.

Darkness closed in around Ben as he crossed to the barn, checked inside, made a pass around the outside and the perimeter of the other outbuildings.

When he was satisfied there were no intruders, he climbed the steps to the house and went straight to his room. He grabbed fresh jeans and a clean shirt and ducked into the bathroom down the hall.

When he emerged, he peeked in at Lily, who lay sound asleep, her puppy in a box beside her bed, also asleep.

Sounds from the kitchen drew him down the stairs when he should have gone straight to bed.

Kate stood with her back to him at the kitchen counter, wearing a worn T-shirt and frayed denim shorts, and she was barefoot. Her hair hung in limp, wet strands, dampening the back of her shirt. "You can wash your hands in the sink, here. Your plate will be ready in a moment."

Knowing it was a mistake, yet unable to help himself, he crossed to the sink and stood beside her. He squirted dish soap onto his fingers and cleaned his already clean hands. He couldn't resist any excuse to be closer to her.

As he dried his hands, she smiled at him.

"Sit. Cara Jo left after reading two books to Lily. Mrs. Henderson left the best roast beef and potatoes you've ever tasted warming in the oven. I'll have a plate full for you in two shakes."

Kate stood within reach and, if he was right, she wasn't wearing a bra. Dear God, he wanted her.

Ben swallowed hard and backed up several steps. "I'm not hungry." For food.

When she turned with a heaping plate in one hand and a glass of iced tea in the other, she frowned. "No argument. You need to eat." She set the plate and glass on the table and pointed at the chair. "Sit."

Too tired to argue, or maybe just too tired to fight it, he sat in the designated chair. Two candles stood in the middle of the table with a box of matches beside them. Ben struck the tip of a match against the matchbox and applied the flame to the wick.

"Sorry, forgot the silverware." Kate dived for a drawer, pulling out a knife, fork and spoon. She hit the light switch on the wall, plunging the room into an intimate hazy glow.

She returned to his side and leaned over him to place the utensils beside his plate.

He couldn't take anymore. He grabbed her around the waist and sat her in his lap. "Do you have any idea what you're doing to me?"

Her eyes widened, her mouth opened in an O, and her cheeks turned a pretty pink. She sucked in a breath and let it out, her blush deepening. "Based on where I'm sitting, I could hazard a pretty good guess."

"Damn it, Kate, I promised it wouldn't happen again."

She sighed. "Some promises were meant to be broken." Her gaze dropped to his lips.

Her words, the way she said them, and that shift of her attention was his undoing. "What am I supposed to do with you? You set me on fire."

Her lips turned upward and she smiled. "Burn, baby, burn."

Laughter rumbled up inside him. He fought the happiness, fought to control a surge of hope. In the end, he lost and grasped her cheeks between his hands, kissing her like she was the buoy that would bring him back to the surface of the sea of sorrow he'd been wallowing in since Sarah's and Julia's deaths.

Her fingers plied loose the buttons on the front of his shirt, one by one. She didn't break the kiss until the last button was freed.

Ben's hands slipped beneath her shirt and up her back. As he'd suspected, she wasn't wearing a bra. Heat rushed to his loins, his member straining against his fly.

Kate shoved the shirt over his shoulders and down his arms.

Ben's fingers slid along her sides and upward to cup her breasts. When his fingers found the taut nipples, he paused. "Lily?"

"Will sleep until morning." She kissed his chin, her lips sliding downward to caress his neck, her breasts pressing into his palms.

Even the child conspired against Ben. With nothing but his memories standing in his way, Ben lost the fight. He shrugged the shirt off his arms and lifted the hem of Kate's T-shirt up and over her head, flinging it across the table. Then he lifted her, spreading her legs wide to straddle his hips. In the soft candlelight he gazed down at her, drinking her in like a man dying of thirst.

"Don't stop now." She raised his hand to her breast. "I'm not good at starting over. I married my high school sweetheart. I don't know how to flirt. I never had any practice."

"You're doing a hell of a job." He rolled her rosy nipples between his thumbs and forefingers.

Her back arched, her hair slipping down to her waist, curling as it dried.

"You should eat." She gasped as he took one nipple between his teeth and nipped.

"I am."

"Food, silly." Her fingers wrapped around his head and held him where he was, her thighs tightening against his sides.

"The only thing I'm hungry for is you." He stood, bringing her up with him, wrapping her thighs around his middle.

Her arms circled his neck as she spread kisses along the column of his throat.

Ben carried her up the stairs to her bedroom, kicking the door open softly so as not to disturb Lily and Pickles.

He set her on her feet and stripped her shorts down her long legs.

Kate stood for a moment, bathed in moonlight peeking through the window. Her tongue swept across her lips, her gaze traveling over him and downward. "You're a bit overdressed." Her fingers closed around the metal rivet of his jeans. She pushed it through the hole and slid the zipper downward, slowly, her fingers brushing against his erection.

Past rational thought, he swung Kate up into his arms and, one-handed, flung back the comforter.

About to lay her against the sheets, he paused.

A movement out of the corner of his eye and a dry rattling sound shot adrenaline through him and he jumped back.

"What? Oh, my God!" Kate clung to him, her arms clamped around his neck, her gaze on the bed. "Is that what I think that is?"

Coiled against the cool white sheets was the biggest rattlesnake Ben had ever encountered. And it was angry.

Chapter Twelve

Kate stifled a scream as she clung to Ben, holding her arms and legs as far away from the snake as she could. She'd have crawled over Ben's body and run if he hadn't been gripping her so tightly. "Do something," she cried.

Ben chuckled, struggling to maintain his hold on her squirming body. "I have to put you down before I can take care of the snake." He strode to the door. "Turn on the light."

Kate flipped the light switch.

The snake on the bed rattled again, perhaps angry at having his sleep disturbed.

Kate shot a glance all around them, searching for friends of the snake in her bed. The floor appeared clear of any other slithering creatures. "Put me down."

Ben dropped her feet to the floor and steadied her. "Are you okay?"

She crossed her arms over her breasts. "No. There's a snake in my bed. A poisonous one at that."

"You can wait in the hall if you like."

"No." She didn't want to leave Ben's side. If anyone could handle a tough situation, it was Ben. "What are you going to do?"

"Get rid of the snake," he said, his tone matter-of-fact.

"How?"

He didn't answer. Instead he approached the end of the

bed, careful to stay out of striking range of the big rattler. He pulled the top sheet and comforter completely off the bed and shook them.

Nothing fell out.

Kate lunged for the sheet and shook it again, before wrapping it around her body.

Ben eased the elastic corners of the fitted sheet off the end of the bed. Circling wide, he repeated the process on the other end of the bed, then he gathered the ends and pulled them together quickly before the snake could slither out and onto the floor.

Carrying the fitted sheet like a bag, he held it away from his body and descended the stairs.

Kate followed, checking the floor before she took every step. She stopped at the top of the stairs, shivering in the air-conditioning.

Ben continued down, stepping out the front door onto the porch. "I'll be back. Don't touch anything until I can check your room over."

Kate held her breath until Ben returned, letting it out as he appeared again in the doorway.

"The snake?"

He closed the door and glanced up at her. "Dead."

Kate heaved a sigh. "Thank God." Then her heart thumped against her ribs. "Lily." She dashed into her daughter's room, slapping the light switch on the wall.

Ben burst through the doorway behind Kate.

Kate gathered Lily up in her arms and held her while Ben checked her bedding and room thoroughly.

"Mommy?"

"Shh, baby. Go back to sleep."

Pickles whined in his box.

"Can Pickles sleep with me?" she asked, her voice groggy, a fist rubbing over her eyes.

"No, baby. Pickles has his own bed."

"I want Pickles to sleep—" A huge yawn interrupted Lily's protest. She snuggled down in Kate's arms and fell back to sleep.

The puppy turned around in his box three times and dropped down, his head draped over his paws.

Ben straightened the bedding and waited for Kate to lay the child down. Afterward, he tucked the sheets around Lily and pressed a kiss to her forehead.

Kate swallowed hard on a knot in her throat.

Ben had kissed Lily, the gesture so natural and right it took Kate's breath away.

When he straightened, his gaze met hers. He nodded toward the door.

Kate stepped out into the hallway, tugging the sheet up securely over her breasts, embarrassed about her behavior. She'd more or less encouraged Ben to make love to her. Hell, she'd practically thrown herself at him. Her cheeks burning, she pulled the door halfway closed and turned toward her bedroom.

Two steps in that direction and she stopped, a huge tremor shaking her so hard her teeth rattled.

Ben's hands settled on her bare shoulders. "What's wrong?"

"I can't go back in there."

"I'll check it out."

"Thanks, but it won't make a difference. I won't be sleeping in there tonight."

"I've disposed of the snake."

"Yeah, but you can't take the image out of my head."

"You can sleep in my room."

"No. You need your sleep more than I do."

"We both need sleep." He cupped her elbow with his warm, strong palm and led her past Lily's room to his.

Once inside the doorway, Kate stopped and stared at the

four-poster bed, images of a naked Ben flashing through her mind. "No. I can't do it."

"I'll sleep on the couch downstairs."

"I can sleep on the couch."

"And if something happened to you downstairs, I might not hear anything."

Kate trembled. "I just won't sleep then."

"Don't be ridiculous. Take the bed." He urged her forward, stripped the comforter back and checked the sheets. "See? No snake."

A shiver racked her body yet again. "I can't get that rattler out of my mind. I almost crawled into bed with a snake." She shivered again.

He shoved a hand through his hair. "If it helps, I'll stay with you until you go to sleep."

She glanced at him, her brows pulling downward. "What we were about to do…"

"Don't worry. I'll only stay until you go to sleep. Nothing else."

"I don't know."

"For crissakes." Ben scooped her up in his arms and tossed her on the bed. "Go to sleep before I forget myself again." He turned his back on her and paced the floor.

Kate adjusted the sheet around her body and moved to the farthest side of the bed. "And I'm supposed to sleep while you pace?" She shook her head.

He stopped and shoved a hand through his hair. The button on his fly remained undone, the zipper halfway down.

Despite her best promise to herself, Kate's gaze zeroed in on the dark hairs peeking through. The shivers of dread for the snake changed to the shivers of the kind of excitement she'd felt before the snake had come on scene.

Her gaze rose to capture Ben's, staring down at her.

He groaned. "I can't do this."

"Then don't." Kate fluffed the comforter, checking beneath it one more time before she settled in, her eyes wide. She turned her back to Ben and feigned sleep. After a moment or two, a sensation of something crawling across her leg made her sit up in the bed and drag her legs up to her chin. She shook the blanket again. Nothing fell out or slithered across the bed.

Kate peered over the top of her sheet-covered knees. "Why are you still standing there? The couch is downstairs. I don't need you." Her voice trailed off. The hell she didn't need him. It was destined to be a long, scary night.

His hand rose to the light switch. "Want me to turn out the light?"

Her hand went up immediately. "No!"

Ben sighed, crossed the room and sat on the edge of the bed.

"What are you doing?"

"Going out of my mind. What does it look like?" He swung his legs, jeans and all up onto the bed. "Come here." Ben gathered her in his arms, pulling her body up against his. "Go to sleep."

"I can't."

"Yes, you can. Close your eyes and picture Lily playing with her puppy."

Snuggled against Ben, one hand resting on his bare chest, Kate tried. Instead of her daughter, all she could imagine was trailing that hand across his taut muscles, finding and pinching the hard little brown nipples.

She closed her eyes, inhaling the fresh, clean scent of soap and man. Her hand slipped over a rib, then another, inching south to the waistband of his jeans.

Ben captured her hand. "This can only lead to one thing."

"You think?"

In a flash, he shoved her onto her back, pinning her wrists above her head. "I loved my wife, Kate. I don't need another woman in my life."

"Then why are you lying on top of me." Her gaze met his unflinchingly. She arched her back, her pelvis rubbing against the hard ridge beneath his jeans. "And why are you so aroused?"

He closed his eyes, his breath coming in short, ragged pants. Then his mouth descended on hers. His hands found the edge of the sheet over her breasts and yanked it downward, peeling it from her body, until she lay naked and trembling. Not out of fear, but in anticipation of what would come next.

She raised a hand to his zipper, sliding it lower until his erection sprang free, hard and straight.

"I didn't want this to happen," he said through gritted teeth.

"So noted." Kate's hand circled him, sliding along his length, dipping inside the denim to cup him, massaging his member. "What are you going to do about it?"

He leaped from the bed and stood with his back to her, breathing hard.

She rose behind him, her hands caressing a path, curving around his shoulders, down his sides to his narrow hips. Kate circled around to his front, beyond caring what he thought of her brazen behavior, beyond patient...ready to take him inside her.

She wanted him to fill the void she'd been living with for so long.

Kate pushed his jeans over his hips and down his legs, her hands caressing his buttocks, his thighs and the sharply defined calves.

He stepped free of the denim and threaded his hands in her hair, dragging her to her feet.

She let him, her body sliding up his, skin-to-delicious-skin. Every nerve ending burned, fire radiating from her core outward.

He cupped the back of her thighs and lifted her, wrapping her legs around his waist. "Stop me now."

"I can't." She wove her fingers into his hair, dragging his head downward until their lips met. "I need you."

His member nudged her opening, the tip sliding in. "Wait."

"Really?" Her thighs tightened around him, lifting her up.

"I have protection in the nightstand…by the bed." He groaned and lifted her off him, laying her across the bed, her legs draped over the side.

Kate reached into the drawer and removed a strip of foil-packaged condoms. She tore the packet open with her teeth and rolled the condom over him, her hand cupping him at the base.

Ben stepped between her legs, grabbed her wrists and pinned them over her head, his erection poised at her entrance. "You make me hotter than the Texas sun."

"That makes two of us, then." She wrapped her legs around his waist and tightened, driving him in.

He slid all the way inside, the smooth, slick sensations so erotic, he threw his head back and drew in a deep, steadying breath.

Then he pulled back out and slammed in again, settling into a fast, smooth rhythm.

As the friction increased, heat built and tingling sensations rippled through Kate's body. Her back arched off the bed, her thighs clenching with each thrust until she pitched over the edge, crying out his name.

His fingers dug into her hips as he plunged in one last time. Ben held steady, his face tense, his muscles bunched and his member throbbing against her channel.

As they tumbled back to the earth, Kate's legs disengaged from around his waist and dropped over the side of the bed.

Ben eased her up on the mattress and lay beside her, spooning her body with his.

"Stay with me?" she begged.

His hand rested on her naked hip. "As long as there are no regrets in the morning."

She sighed. "No regrets." Kate snuggled in his arms, feeling more safe and secure than she had since her husband left for war. If only she could count on this to last.

Sadly, she knew she couldn't.

A single tear slid down her cheek and dropped onto the sheet. How could a man come to mean so much to her in such a short time? Was she desperate for male companionship? Or was it *this* man that made her feel this way?

It didn't matter. When his replacement came, Ben would leave. She'd be on her own again.

But for now, he kept the boogeyman and the snakes away while warming her backside.

Kate closed her eyes and fell asleep.

BEN LAY FOR a long time, his arms around Kate's naked body, holding her like they belonged together. Making love to a woman had that effect on him. That had to be the explanation for his sudden desire to stay with her, to become a part of her and Lily's lives.

But that wouldn't be fair to either one of them. He'd had a wife and daughter. He'd loved them both so much it still hurt to think about them. How could he begin to love someone else as much? He couldn't. It wasn't possible. Was it?

Kate stirred against him, her bottom brushing sensitive areas, stirring desire so strong he couldn't suppress it.

He'd asked Hank to find his replacement. What if he did? Could Ben walk away and leave Kate in the hands of someone else? Could he trust that other agent to take care of Kate and Lily, to protect them from whoever was after them?

His arms tightened around Kate, his chest squeezing tight. He couldn't desert them. Not now. Not when they needed him most.

The sound of a puppy's cries pulled Ben from his thoughts. Pickles had to be missing his mother.

Ben slipped out of the bed and stood, gazing down at Kate as she lay deep in sleep, caressed by the moonlight streaming through the window. Her long hair looking more auburn in this light as it splayed across the pillow, her lips parted as if she fell asleep whispering.

Ben brushed a strand of hair from her cheek and bent to press his lips to hers.

"Sweet dreams."

He slipped into his jeans and zipped them, then padded barefoot to the next room.

Lily lay splayed across her bed, her foot dangling over the side.

Pickles looked up at Ben, his soulful blue eyes begging Ben to rescue him from his grief and loneliness.

Ben scooped up the puppy and the box and headed down the stairs to the couch. He understood how Pickles felt. Torn from the ones he loved, but surrounded by the possibility of a new family.

In the night, everything seemed more overwhelming than during the light of day.

As he lay on the couch, his feet hanging over the arms, Ben cuddled the puppy against him and turned over the day's events in his mind.

Two things stood out, touching him with a cold hand of dread.

A gang of coyotes was using the Flying K as a place to traffic human cargo.

Secondly, that snake hadn't gotten into Kate's bed on its own. Someone had put it there.

Chapter Thirteen

Kate yawned, stretched and glanced around her room, disoriented at first. Her tender breasts rubbed against the sheet and she remembered where she was—in Ben's bed—and that she was naked.

"Mommy?" Lily called out.

Kate scrambled to her feet, wondering where Ben had gone. She had just wrapped the sheet around her body when Lily ran by the open door.

"Mommy?"

Her frightened cry spurred Kate forward. "Lily, I'm here."

Lily stopped at the top of the stairs and looked back. "Where's Pickles? He's not in his box."

Kate smiled and shrugged, relieved her daughter hadn't asked why she was in a different room and wrapped in a sheet. "I don't know. Let me get dressed and I'll help you find him."

"Lily?" Ben's deep voice echoed up the stairs.

Kate moved to peer over the banister railing at the man.

He stood barefoot, wearing nothing but his jeans. The sight of his naked chest sent Kate's pulse skittering into crazy palpitations. An image of herself lying naked with him spread warmth throughout her body, and extra fire to one place in particular.

He shot a heated glance at her before he held the puppy up for Lily to see. "I have Pickles down here."

"Pickles." Lily ran down the stairs, her hand trailing along the railing, wild, light red hair flying out around her shoulders.

A sharp tug in the region of her heart made Kate press a hand to her chest. How like a family they were. She had to remind herself that it was nothing but an illusion. A fantasy bubble destined to pop when life returned to normal.

Ben handed Lily the puppy. "I've already taken him outside. He should play all right inside for a few minutes. Stay in the house, please."

"I will." Lily set the puppy on the floor and ran into the living room, squealing as Pickles chased after her, barking in his shrill puppy voice.

Which left Ben staring up at Kate. He stepped up one of the stair risers. "How are you this morning?"

Kate gathered the sheet around her body, a flush of warmth burning up her neck into her cheeks. "I'm fine."

He climbed two more steps, his gaze pinning hers. "Any regrets?"

Her eyes widened, her heart pounding so hard, she could hear it banging against her eardrums. "No regrets." She swallowed hard and forced herself to ask, "And you?"

When Ben cleared the top step and stood with her on the landing, Kate stepped away until her back bumped against the wall.

"None." Ben advanced slowly. When he stopped, barefoot and toe to toe with her, he reached out and touched the rise of her breasts above the sheet. "Seems you were wearing this last night."

A smile fluttered across her lips, shyness weighing on her words. "I think I need a new outfit."

"I kind of like this one." His fingers tugged on the end, untucking the edges.

Kate inhaled, her breasts rising as Ben unfolded the sheet, exposing her body to his piercing gaze.

"Oh, yes. I like this outfit." He bent, capturing a nipple between his teeth, nipping lightly.

Kate's hands feathered through his hair, pressing against the back of his neck. She closed her eyes, letting the rampant waves of desire swarm over her.

"Mommy?" Lily's voice brought her back to earth with a jolt.

Kate jerked the sheet closed, stepped around Ben and leaned over the railing. "What is it, Lily?"

"Pickles had an accident."

A chuckle rose up her throat. "I'll be down in a moment to help you clean it up." When she turned toward her bedroom, Ben blocked her path. She blinked up at him. "You heard Lily, the puppy had an acci—"

Ben lifted her chin with a crooked finger and kissed her hard, his tongue darting out to capture hers in a brief caress.

As quickly as he'd possessed her, he let her go. "I'll take care of the puppy." Then he left her on the landing and padded down the steps, entering the living room in search of Lily.

Kate stood still for several seconds, unable to get her bearings. Hell, she'd been unable to form coherent thoughts since Ben had come into her life. If she wasn't careful, she'd fall in love with a man who still loved his dead wife. And where would that leave her?

Kate eased into her bedroom, on the lookout for anything that slithered or rattled. The room remained silent as she dressed for the day in jeans, a white button-down shirt and cowboy boots. She pulled out the key her father's attorney had given her at the reading of the will and decided it was time to look for whatever it belonged to.

Perhaps when she found the lock, it would unveil the reason why someone wanted her off the property and away from Wild Oak Canyon.

As Kate gathered her ponytail in place, corralling her wild curls with a rubber band, the telephone at the bottom of the stairs rang. She decided to forgo makeup. It wasn't as if she was trying to impress anyone. Certainly not Ben. He wasn't sticking around. What had happened last night wasn't the stuff relationships were made of. Ben was a bodyguard. Kate was the job. When she no longer needed his protection, he'd be gone.

If she was smart, she'd discontinue this sex-only connection with the bodyguard. It wasn't fair to her, to Lily or to him.

With a deep breath, she hurried down the stairs and lifted the phone on the fourth ring. "Hello."

"Kate, it's Cara Jo."

"Hi." Kate's heart warmed at the sound of her new friend's voice.

"Just wanted to let you know the local church in Wild Oak Canyon has a Mother's Day Out program. Lily might enjoy playing with children her own age a couple times a week."

"Wow, that would be great. What days?"

"Tuesdays and Thursdays from nine until three o'clock." Cara Jo called out to someone on her end of the phone.

"Are you at the diner?" Kate asked.

"I am. It being Thursday, I thought I'd let you know early enough to get Lily in today, if you had a mind to." She chuckled softly. "Purely selfish reasons, I assure you. If you come to town, you could join me for lunch and do a little shopping without having to drag poor Lily around."

"That sounds good. I could run by the sheriff's office again and report the dead cattle, for all the good it would do."

Cara Jo snorted. "At least you'd have a record of it."

"Right." Kate glanced at Lily playing on the floor in the

living room with Pickles. The little puppy had as much energy as the four-year-old.

Nothing like jumping into the community. And Lily was used to playing with the children she'd met at the day care in Houston. Kate made the decision. "I'll check it out today. If all goes well, I'll meet you for lunch."

"Make it around eleven-thirty. Twelve to one-thirty is our busy time and it gets hard to find a seat."

"Will do." Kate hung up, ran back up the stairs and grabbed play clothes, shoes, barrettes and a hairbrush from Lily's room.

When she returned to the first floor, the living room was empty.

Sounds of voices and laughter came from the kitchen.

When Kate entered, she was struck by how natural the scene appeared.

Lily sat in a chair on a stack of books, digging into a bowl of cereal. Ben sat beside her with a plate of eggs, bacon and toast. Mrs. Henderson busied herself at the stove, talking to both of them with her back to the room.

Kate smiled. "Good morning."

"Oh, Kate, dear. Sit. I have breakfast for you." Mrs. Henderson lifted a fry pan full of fluffy, yellow scrambled eggs and faced her. "Did you sleep well?"

Kate's face heated. "Yes. I did." *Minus the snake and the musical beds and making love to Ben.* She had slept well once she'd fallen asleep in Ben's arms. She refused to meet his gaze, but out of the corner of her eye she could see the way his lips twitched.

If he smiled now, she'd throw something at him.

Instead he shoved a forkful of eggs into his mouth and chewed.

"Lily, how would you like to make some new friends today?" Kate asked, hoping to pull attention off her red cheeks and focus it on her baby girl.

Lily set her spoon beside her bowl and lifted her cup of milk. "Yes, please."

Kate continued for Ben's benefit, "There's a Mother's Day Out program at the local church. Cara Jo from the diner suggested it, thinking Lily might like to meet some of the local children. I think it's a good idea."

Ben nodded. "Eddy had a few things he'd like picked up in town. We can take the truck."

"I'll take my car, you can follow. I think I'll be safe in town and I might want to do a little shopping while there."

Ben frowned. "Are you sure you don't want me to drive?"

"I don't think it's necessary." Kate remained firm. If Ben was leaving, she needed to get around on her own and not be afraid. "Nothing's going to happen in a town full of people."

Ben's brows didn't rise. "I'm not thrilled with the idea of taking two vehicles. Seems a waste of fuel and time. But as long as you wait for me to follow you back to the ranch, I suppose it's okay."

Kate almost smiled. For some strange reason, she liked pushing his buttons. But she understood his reasons. It was his job to protect her and Lily. "I'll let you know when I'm ready to head home."

Fifteen minutes later, she'd finished her breakfast, brushed her teeth and Lily's, and gathered her keys and purse.

Ben waited outside beside his truck, his brows dented in what appeared to be a permanent frown. He'd already switched the booster seat into the backseat of her car.

Lily ran to his arms. "Pickles cried when I put him in the box."

"Mrs. Henderson will let him out to play once we leave. He'll be fine until you get home." Ben tucked her into the safety seat and buckled the belt over her lap, then pressed a kiss to her forehead.

Kate stood back, once again amazed at how comfortable

the two were together. Already, she predicted it would be hard on Lily when Ben left.

Kate climbed into the car and pulled out onto the highway bound for the little town and the church where Lily would spend the day doing what kids did—play.

The drive was uneventful and Kate relished the time alone with Lily. It gave her the opportunity to think through what had happened the night before. She never would have thought she'd be so quickly attracted to a man, and never had she dreamed she'd jump into bed with a stranger after knowing him such a short time. Having married her high school sweetheart, Kate hadn't dated as an adult. One thing was for sure, she wasn't setting a good example for Lily. Still she didn't regret the magic she'd experienced with Ben the night before.

Kate parked in front of the church.

Ben parked on the passenger side of Kate's car. He got to Lily before Kate and lifted the child out onto the ground, tucking her hand in his.

Kate took Lily's other hand and they walked into the church together.

At the administrative office, Kate filled out paperwork and let them make a copy of Lily's shot records. When it came to filling out the emergency data card, she paused. She wrote down her home phone number and her cell phone number, but the cell number was only reliable sometimes. "If you can't get me on my cell phone, call Cara Jo's diner and ask for me or leave a message with Cara Jo. I'll check in there."

"Leave my cell number, too, as backup." Ben recited his number and Kate wrote it on the form.

Kate and Ben walked with the administrator to the classroom Lily would be in. Six children ranging in age from three to five gathered around tables, wearing cute little aprons. They were elbow-deep in finger painting.

Lily was so excited, she didn't even say goodbye.

Kate left the building, happy that her daughter would have a fun-filled day with children her age.

"Now what?" Ben asked.

"I want to stop by the county assessor, do a little shopping and then meet Cara Jo for lunch." She shot a glance his way, but didn't linger on his handsome face, afraid she'd ask him to stay with her. "What about you?"

"While you're in town, I can take care of reporting the dead cattle to the sheriff's office. At least get it on record. I need to run out to Hank's and check on the status of that DVD. Then I'll drop by the hardware store for the items Eddy needed for the ranch."

Kate glanced at her watch. "Meet back here at three?"

"Three." He caught Kate's arm as she turned away. "Don't go anywhere else without notifying me first, will you?"

"I won't." Her arm tingled where he touched her. Damn. The man had her tied in knots and wanting so much more. Things she shouldn't be thinking in broad daylight came to mind more than she cared to admit. With her thoughts on her bodyguard, she wasn't focusing on what was important. The nutcase causing her grief and the human trafficking happening on her own land.

"Three o'clock." She scooted away from his grip on her arm and climbed into her car. After shifting into Reverse, she left the parking lot, cranking the air conditioner up to chill her suddenly flaming cheeks.

She stopped by the county tax assessor's office to discover no change in the computer situation. They expected someone out that afternoon to work on it.

After she left the county offices, Kate spent thirty minutes in the General Store, exploring the aisles, getting familiar with what Wild Oak Canyon had to offer. It wasn't a huge department store, but they sold jeans, chambray shirts and cowboy hats. That and a few odds and ends in fencing supplies and plain pantry staples, fresh bread and milk. After she'd gone up and down each aisle, it was time to meet with Cara Jo at the diner across the street from the General Store.

When Kate pushed through the diner's door, Cara Jo dashed by her, carrying three heaping plates of food.

"Sorry, one of my waitresses called in sick. I have to work the lunch crowd." She set the plates on a table in the corner where three men dressed in jeans and chambray shirts sat with their forks and knives ready to dig in.

On her way back past Kate, Cara Jo gave her an apologetic frown. "Sorry. Can we do a rain check on our lunch?"

"That's fine. I ate breakfast not long ago."

"Oh, please sit, have lunch. It's on me." Cara Jo whooshed by and grabbed another two plates from the window into the kitchen.

Kate glanced around at the busy establishment. She didn't want to sit by herself, and she didn't feel like sitting with strangers.

Robert Sanders occupied a booth near the far corner, sitting across the table from the sheriff, their heads bent close, intense expressions on their faces.

Kate didn't see herself getting into a conversation with the two men. And they appeared to be discussing business. She caught Cara Jo on her next pass. "I'm going to head out to the ranch. I have some things to do out there. I'll be back in town around three to get Lily. I'll stop by then for a cup of coffee, if you have time."

"Oh, sure. Three will be our slow time. I'll see you then." Cara Jo was off again, snatching up a carafe of steaming coffee and a pitcher of ice water.

Kate left the diner and stood outside on the sidewalk. She dug her cell phone out of her purse and dialed Ben's number. The call went straight to his voice mail. She left a message, or at least hoped she did. With spotty reception, she wasn't sure she stayed connected throughout her call.

With nothing else to do, not feeling like shopping and

with nobody to talk to, Kate decided to do what she'd told Cara Jo she was going to do and head back out to the ranch.

Lily would be happily playing with her new friends and Ben was busy doing errands and updating the sheriff's deputies and Hank Derringer.

A little lonely and a bit anxious, Kate couldn't stand around and wait for someone to show up or free up to babysit her. She still had a lot of unpacking to do. Mrs. Henderson would be there and now that Kate knew how to handle the Glock, she would be just fine.

Kate jammed her hand into her jeans pocket, searching for her car keys and found the mystery key her father had left her.

She could spend time searching the house and surrounding outbuildings for the lock the key belonged to. Kate climbed into her car and headed out of town to the ranch. The wind had picked up, buffeting her little car around. With few trees or hills to block the wind, it blew through, hard and fast and filled with fine grains of sand that pinged against the windshield.

In broad daylight, Kate didn't expect to be accosted. But then she hadn't expected a biker gang to show up in her front yard the first morning after she'd arrived. Just to play it safe, Kate kept alternating watching the pavement ahead and behind in the rearview mirrors. Anytime she passed a road connecting to the highway, she studied it carefully, looking for suspicious vehicles, lurking, waiting for her to pass by, alone and vulnerable.

She'd be glad when she got back to the ranch with Mrs. Henderson and Eddy.

Kate gripped the steering wheel so tightly, her knuckles turned white as she struggled to quell her rising fears and to maintain control of the little car being tossed around by strong southerly winds.

By the time she drove through the gate and up to the ranch house, Kate's fingers were cramping. And all for what? Nothing happened on the highway and no biker gang greeted her at the house.

As Kate climbed out of the car, her hair escaped its neat ponytail and whipped around her face and neck.

A rumbling-on-gravel sound made her turn and face the driveway she'd driven in on. Another vehicle turned off the county road onto the gravel drive far enough away that she couldn't make it out, but close enough to send a flash of fear through her.

Her brows furrowed, Kate hurried toward the house, scraping her mind for the location of the pistol and shells.

"Oh, good. You're here." Mrs. Henderson met her at the screen door, her purse hooked over her shoulder. "Mr. Henderson forgot to tell me he had an appointment at the clinic today and the Customs and Border Protection folks called a while ago to say they were on the way out to check on your reports of lights and dead cattle. I'd stick around and answer their questions, but now that you're here…"

"How long did the CBP say they'd be before they got here?" Kate asked.

"There they are now." Mrs. Henderson pointed down the drive.

The vehicle Kate had seen came into view. A big, white Hummer H2, with knobby tires and a green stripe, spit up a wide cloud of dust on the gravel drive.

"When they called about an hour ago, I thought it would be no problem. Eddy said he'd meet them at the barn when they came in. I had just pulled a pie out of the oven when David called to say he was picking me up." The older woman glanced over Kate's shoulder. "That should be Dave now. I wasn't sure what to do with the puppy when I left so it's a good thing you showed up when you did." She gave Kate a half smile. "Sorry. My husband can be forgetful. That's why I go to his appointments with him."

"Don't worry. I'll be fine without you."

Her eyes narrowed and she looked past Kate. "Where's Mr. Harding?"

"He'll be along in a bit," Kate fudged. No use detaining Marge when her husband had already driven out to pick her up.

"I can't leave you alone. Mr. Henderson will just have to go on without me." Marge let the purse slide down her arm and turned in the doorway.

"No, really. I'll be fine. Eddy's around here. The Border Protection is here. And if that's not enough, Ben gave me lessons on how to fire my pistol. It turns out I'm a pretty good shot. You go on with Mr. Henderson. He needs you more than I do."

The older woman's brows dipped. "Are you sure?" She glanced around the immediate vicinity of the ranch house as if expecting someone to be lurking in the shadows. "I don't feel right leaving you like this."

Kate rested her hand on Mrs. Henderson's arm. "You don't have to baby me. I can handle myself and Ben will be along shortly."

"Okay. But do be careful." She squeezed Kate's hand and descended the stairs. "I'll be back to fix dinner around five."

"Don't make the trip out again. I can cook, you know." Another near lie. She wasn't that good, but Mrs. Henderson didn't have to know that.

Marge patted her purse. "Well, then, I'll see you in the morning."

"Thanks, Mrs. H." Kate sighed as Mr. Henderson got out of the driver's seat and rounded the front of the car to open the door for his wife. He waved at Kate and climbed back into the car and turned it around, headed back to the highway and town.

Kate admired the way the old couple relied on each other for things. They loved each other, which was evident in the way the old man took care of Marge and she him.

When Troy had been alive, Kate had never quite pictured them growing old together. Now she supposed that she'd never had enough time on her hands to dwell on such things, what with her pregnancy occurring so close to when they'd gotten married and then Troy leaving before even Kate knew she was with child.

Kate stood in the yard as the officers stepped out of their SUV and strode across the ground to her.

One of the officers held out his hand. "I'm Officer Mendoza with U.S. Customs and Border Protection. Are you Ms. Langsdon?"

"Yes, that's me."

"We're here to review recent reports of suspicious activity in the area."

"I take it the helicopters didn't find the two trucks last night?"

"No, ma'am." The spokesman of the two pulled a notepad out of his pocket. "Could you or your husband show me where you saw the dead cattle?"

Kate let the husband comment pass by without comment. "Your best bet will be to have my foreman show you where you can find the dead cattle and the ravine where we saw the two trucks."

Eddy chose that moment to cross the barnyard, slapping his cowboy hat against his leg, dust rising and whipping away with the wind.

Kate brought the CBP officers up to date on what had happened on the ranch, from the attack in the house, the home intrusions, biker gangs and dead cattle to the truckloads of people.

Mendoza shook his head. "I suggest you get a good guard dog and a bodyguard."

"Got the bodyguard. Working on the guard dog." Her lips curved as an image of Ben came to mind and at the thought of Pickles being a guard dog.

Mendoza glanced over her shoulder and around the yard. "A bodyguard isn't much good if he's not around to guard you."

"He's on his way back from town," Kate lied, realizing she'd been stupid to leave Wild Oak Canyon without him. Without Marge as backup she only had Eddy to protect her should someone cause trouble.

When Kate had told them all she knew, she paused, waiting for their response.

Officer Mendoza closed his notepad and slid it into his shirt pocket. "Could you show me where you found the carcasses?"

Kate turned to Eddy.

"Sí." Eddy eyed the men. "I have extra horses in the barn."

The officer smiled. "Thanks, but we'll stick with the SUV. It gets in most places the horses can go."

Eddy didn't respond, his gaze roving over the huge tires and fancy paint job of the CBP vehicle. Then he shrugged. "You'll have to follow me and my horse." He turned and walked away.

Mendoza grinned. "He always so talkative?"

Kate smiled. "He has to warm up to you."

"How long have you owned the Flying K?"

It was Kate's turn to smile. "A grand total of a week."

Eddy had mounted his horse and stood waiting by the gate to the pasture.

"Guess we better get going." Mendoza nodded at Kate. "Thank you for your time."

"Hope you find the trucks. I'm worried about the passengers as hot as it gets out here." Kate watched as the Hummer cleared the gate and Eddy closed it behind them.

Once the group disappeared across the pasture, Kate dug the key from her pocket and performed a systematic search of the inside of the house, fitting the little key into every lock on the off chance it was the right one. She checked behind furniture, paintings and beneath rugs for any hidden doors.

The attic had been particularly creepy, with spiderwebs and a thick layer of dust. The hot Texas sun had heated the top of the house so much Kate had broken into a sweat as soon as she'd pulled down the attic access door and climbed to the top. After checking out two old trunks and an antique desk, she retreated to the air-conditioned second floor.

She let the attic door close on its springs. So far she'd struck out on finding the lock inside the house. She headed out the front door, letting the screen slap closed behind her.

Living in Houston had conditioned Kate to the constant noise of urban life. Here, the silence was only interrupted by the wail of wind against the windows. When she stepped out on the porch, the strong westerly breeze hit her with a heated blast, slapping her hair around her head. As far as Kate knew, she was the only person within miles of the ranch house. That gave her a kind of lonely, distant feeling. A quick glance at her watch told her she didn't have much time to check out the rest of the buildings if she wanted to be back in town on time to pick up Lily at the church and have a cup of coffee with Cara Jo.

She descended the steps, blinking the sand and grit out of her eyes. Choosing the shed closest to the house as a place to start looking, Kate kicked up dust as she trod across the dry Texas soil and flung open the door to the small building. The interior was packed with an ancient riding lawn mower, an antique car probably dating back to the 1940s, a variety of spare parts and equipment, a large rollaway toolbox and fishing poles.

After the bright sunshine, the interior was dark and deeply shadowed. She flipped the light switch beside the door and nothing happened. She'd need a flashlight if she planned to explore in the outbuildings. How long had it been since anyone had been inside this one? At least long enough to accumulate a thick layer of dust. Which, in this part of Texas, could be as little as a day. At the least, she could check out the toolboxes. They appeared to have tiny locks on some of the drawers.

The shed had no windows and only the one large door. Kate opened it wide and leaned a cement block against it to keep the wind from slamming it shut.

Then she stepped through, blocking the sun for a moment. She hugged the shadows, allowing for as much light as possible.

First, she tried the toolboxes. The key didn't fit the two locks, so she moved on. Kate squeezed between the front of the antique car and the wall of the building to get behind it. A scorpion skittered over a concrete block and down the side into a shadow.

Kate hated scorpions, having been stung more than once living in Houston. A shiver slithered across her warm skin. She'd have to warn Lily about the dangers of picking up rocks and things.

On the other side of the antique auto hung a rack of fishing poles. Below the rack, on the dirt floor was a tackle box with a keyhole on the front.

Ready to try anything, Kate stuck the key in the hole and turned it.

The lock clicked open.

A rush of excitement filled her and she dropped to her knees to better see what might be inside. The lighting behind the car was minimal, dust particles gleaming in the air. Kate held her breath as she laid her hands on the box, her pulse hammering through her veins.

Careful to look for scorpions or black widow spiders, she eased the lid back. From all she could see with the shadows and limited light, it was what it looked like. A fishing tackle box. The top compartment was loaded with dusty lures and faded rubber worms.

Kate let go of the breath she'd been holding. "Why would he leave me a key to a fishing tackle box?"

She sat back on her haunches and lifted the top compartment, exposing the bottom of the container.

Once again her breath hitched in her throat. Beneath a filet knife and a pair of pliers lay a mix of lures and lead weights. Buried among them was a slim silver thumb drive.

Was this it? Was this the item the key was hiding? Kate moved the knife and pliers aside and fished the thumb drive out of the box.

She shoved the data storage device into her pocket and stood.

The heavy shed door slammed shut, cutting off the light, throwing Kate into complete darkness. She reached out a hand to steady herself against the antique car and waited for the wind to blow the door open again so that she could see to find her way out.

The door didn't open.

Kate felt her way back around the old car to the front, her shirt catching on a nail protruding from the wall, ripping through the fabric and tearing into her skin. She screamed and nearly tripped over the forgotten concrete block the scorpion had scurried beneath.

Heart racing, afraid she'd brush against something deadly, sharp or creepy, she moved around the wall until her fingers brushed against a hinge. Finally, she'd reached the door.

Wind whistled through the cracks, a dark, lonely sound.

Kate leaned against the door and pushed. It didn't budge. She tried again, this time putting her full weight into it. The door remained closed. She stepped back, tucked her shoulder and slammed into the door. She bounced back.

As the truth dawned on her, her heart sank to her stomach. The door had been locked from the outside.

Chapter Fourteen

Ben sat across the desk from Hank. "That's what's been happening."

"Too much for young Kate to handle alone." Hank nodded. "I'm glad you've been there to protect her." He leaned forward. "I received word from one of my connections in Customs and Border Protection. They found a dead woman on a ranch adjacent to the Flying K two weeks ago. From what they said, she was an illegal immigrant. How she got there, they would only guess. She died of exposure and dehydration."

"Damn." Ben shook his head. "A dead woman, dead cattle, intruders. You think they're trafficking humans across the Flying K and don't want Kate to interfere?"

"Sounds like it. A deadly situation if Kate gets in the middle. The immigrants aren't who she needs to be worried about. It's the coyotes who bring them across. They don't care who they have to kill to get paid."

"Hank, we only saw young women in the backs of those trucks."

Hank glanced up at Ben. "If they're trafficking young women, we have an even bigger problem. Someone stateside is harboring them and possibly selling them to underground sex dens."

Ben clasped his hands together to keep them from shaking. "Like the one we busted in Austin. I caught one of their suppliers, Marcus Mendez. The bastard got off on a technicality, then he came after my family. Think these are connected?"

"Could be." Hank leaned back in his chair. "I spoke with the regional director of the CBP. They didn't find the trucks you and Kate saw last night."

"Damn it." Ben stood and paced in front of Hank's desk. "I should have stopped them there."

"You had Kate to protect and you were outnumbered." Hank rounded his desk and laid a hand on Ben's shoulder. "You did the only thing you could. Now that you know they're running a human trafficking trade across the Flying K, you have to keep Kate from stumbling into them."

"I'll try but she was real upset by what we saw." Kate had a mind of her own and might try something dumb to help those girls. Ben blew out a long breath and dragged a hand through his hair. "I should be with her now."

"Where is she?" Hank asked.

"I left her at the diner. She should be okay there for a little while." Only now he wasn't so sure. Trouble had been following Kate since she'd arrived in this part of Texas. "Before I go, anything on the video?"

"As a matter of fact, we did make a little headway." He clicked the keyboard on his computer and then nodded toward the flat-screen television mounted on the wall behind Ben. "Look at this."

Static filled the screen, then a wavering image of Kyle Kendrick blinked into view.

"Hello, Kate. If you've received this video, something has happened to me and I'm either dead or missing and presumed dead. I couldn't leave without letting you know that of all the regrets in my life, you and your mother are my most heartfelt."

After a short pause, he continued.

"I can't say that I lived a good life. I didn't go to church, I wasn't a pillar of the community and I avoided jail on more occasions than I'd care to remember."

Ben sat back, his heart squeezing in his chest as he imagined Kate watching this video and her reaction to seeing the man on the screen for her first time.

"Then I met your mother and everything changed. I wanted to be a better man. I wanted to make her proud of me, and I thought I could. But I was in too deep. The people I worked with had me. Imagine being married to the mob. In this case, the Mexican Mafia cartels."

Ben whistled, noting the haggard expression, the dark circles around the man's eyes. Eyes that looked so much like a haunted version of Kate's. "What a life."

"I married your mother, thinking I could shake their influence. I thought I could just quit, stop running drugs and start fresh." The man in the video shook his head. "I was wrong and it almost got your mother killed." He ran a hand through his hair and tipped his head back, squeezing shut his eyes. "I had to let her go. To send her away. I didn't know she was pregnant with you. If they'd known how much I cared for her and anything about my unborn child, they'd have used it against me. I couldn't contact you, couldn't talk to your mother. I had to shut the door to that part of my life completely or risk your lives. It was the hardest thing I've done in my entire life."

Kyle Kendrick stared into the camera, his eyes narrowing. "When the DEA cornered me in Vegas, I knew it was over. They would have sent me to jail, which, in retrospect, might have been easier. Instead, they gave me a chance to redeem myself. If I would become their informant, they wouldn't lock me up." Kyle snorted. "I should have let them send me to jail." Kyle shook his head slowly.

"Once I started ratting out the leaders of the cartels, I

knew my days were numbered. But I hung in there, trying to find out who the stateside head honcho was."

Ben shot a glance at Hank.

"I've come so close I might be in trouble. I'm sending this video in case something happens to me. I wanted you to know how much I loved you and your mother."

After another short pause, Kyle continued.

"In the envelope with this video is a key. It unlocks a tackle box you'll find in the shed with the old Cadillac. In the bottom of the tackle box is a flash drive. It contains all the notes I used to nail the members of the cartel and the work I've compiled leading up to the discovery of the state-side crime boss. At the time of this video, I know there are things happening in the area. I leave this information with you in the event of my untimely but fully expected death. The data is encrypted, so you'll need to hand it over to some-one who can break the code. What you do with it is up to you. Toss it, ignore it or hand it off to the DEA, I don't care. Just don't get involved. I would hate to think my work once again puts you in danger."

Ben narrowed his eyes and focused on the screen.

"As I was saying, several factions are active. Drug run-ning and human trafficking. The coyotes who run the peo-ple across the border referred to the stateside connection as *Diablo Patrón,* the devil boss. I think I know who's respon-sible, but haven't accumulated enough evidence to nail him. If what I think is true…" He looked at his hands clasped in between his knees. "Let's just say, I want to verify before I call in the Feds. The stakes are high. Whatever happens to me, know that I deserved what I got. Whatever you do, don't get tangled up in this mess. And watch out for the fol-lowing men…"

As Ben leaned forward, the picture on the screen tilted.

Kyle Kendrick lurched forward to catch the camera, but

missed, and the machine fell to the floor with a loud crash. Then static and gray squiggles filled the video screen.

"Who?" Ben leaped to his feet. "Who was she supposed to look out for?"

Hank stood, as well. "That's the kicker. Nothing else was recorded. Or Kendrick thought he'd finished recording his message and didn't. He must have been in a hurry to get the disk in the mail."

"Holy hell." Ben paced to the end of the French doors and back across Hank's spacious wood-paneled office. He stopped and faced the older man. "She needs to leave now. Go back to Houston, get the hell out of Texas. If the cartel finds out about the flash drive, she's dead."

"Scared the hell out of me, too." Hank walked around the desk and laid a hand on Ben's shoulder. "And there's one other thing I wanted you to know."

Ben looked into Hank's eyes. What else could go wrong?

"I hired another cowboy with the skills necessary to take over for you with the Langsdon woman. You don't have to go back there. He's here on the ranch. I can send him immediately."

Ben pressed a hand to his gut as if he'd been punched. "No."

"Are you sure? He has a stack of medals and credentials almost as impressive as yours."

"No." Ben straightened. God, what was he doing? He had an out. He didn't have to go back to the Flying K and be around Kate, whose body and soul reminded him of all he had to live for. He wouldn't have to face Lily, the child who'd worked her way into his heart in such a short time and left him open to her unconditional love and the heartbreak of leaving her behind when the job was done.

"I'll see this one through," Ben said. He headed for the door before he could change his mind, or before Hank could pull rank on him and change it for him.

"What about the video?"

Ben stopped. "Do you have it in a format I can show Kate?"

"Do you have a computer?"

"Yes."

Hank dropped into his desk chair, plugged a flash drive into the side of his monitor and clicked his keyboard. A moment later he yanked the flash drive from the monitor and handed it to Ben. "Be careful out there. Don't hesitate to call me in or to notify the DEA if things get out of hand."

"Don't worry. I'll be in touch." Ben left, climbing into his truck with a sense of impending doom.

Kate had come to the Flying K with the hope of starting over, of providing a good home for Lily. She'd ended up in a hotbed of danger.

Ben couldn't get back to her fast enough. Thank goodness she'd stayed in town.

The drive back to Wild Oak Canyon passed in a flash, considering Ben broke every speed limit the whole way. Thank goodness the county sheriff couldn't hope to patrol all the roads leading into the community with so few on staff.

Once in town, he pulled into the diner, his gaze searching for and not finding Kate's car. His heart skipped several beats, but he refused to let himself get worked up. He unbuckled his seat belt, dropped down to the pavement and looked around.

Cara Jo stepped out of the diner, her brows furrowed. "Oh, thank goodness you're here."

Ben's adrenaline spiked. "Why? Where's Kate?"

"She left right before lunch to head back to the ranch. She promised to be back in time to pick up Lily, but the woman in charge of the Mother's Day Out program called and said Kate hadn't come and Lily was the last one there. I tried to call you, but you didn't answer. I tried Kate's home phone and there was no answer. I was just about to get Lily myself, but I was afraid I wouldn't be on the list of people allowed to collect her."

Ben was already back in the truck and pulling out of the parking lot by the time Cara Jo finished talking. He whipped out onto the street, drove the few blocks and skidded to a stop in front of the church.

The woman he'd met earlier stepped out the front door of the church, holding Lily's hand. She turned and locked the church.

"Mr. Ben!" Lily jerked her hand free of the woman's and ran toward him, her arms outstretched.

Ben gathered her to him and lifted her off her feet.

"Thank goodness you're here. Lily was upset and worried you had lost your way." The woman looked around Ben. "Is Ms. Langsdon with you?"

"No, she had something come up and asked me to pick up Lily," Ben lied. He held Lily close, his heart aching for the child who'd thought she was forgotten.

Lily leaned back, tear tracks dried on her cheeks. "Can we go home now? Pickles missed me."

Ben nodded. "Yes, we can." He thanked the woman and tucked Lily into the backseat of his truck, buckling the seat belt over her lap. He didn't have the booster seat, but the buckle would have to do until he got back to the ranch and found Kate.

She'd promised not to go back until he could go with her. And why wasn't Mrs. Henderson answering the phone at the ranch?

Questions swirled in his mind throughout the drive out to the Flying K. When he came within sight of the house, he spied Kate's car sitting in the drive.

Nothing moved. No one came out to greet them.

Ben shifted into Park and climbed down. He lifted Lily out of the backseat and carried her to the house. The front door was unlocked. When he pushed it open, he called out, "Kate?"

As soon as he set Lily on her feet, she ran for the kitchen where Pickles's shrill barks created such a loud ruckus, Ben could barely hear himself think.

The house was a disaster. Drawers had been pulled out of the kitchen cabinets, pots and pans lay strewn across the floor.

"Pickles!" Lily cried out. "Where's Pickles?"

A high-pitched whine sounded from behind an overturned chair.

Ben found the puppy's box wedged between a cabinet and the chair and lifted it out, puppy and all.

Lily leaned over the box and let the puppy lick her fingers. "Oh, Pickles, did you miss me?"

Ben checked the pantry and locked the back door, then lifted Lily in his arms. "Sorry, sweetheart, we'll come back for Pickles in a minute."

He didn't want to leave the little girl alone until he was certain whoever had turned the house upside down was no longer there. He carried Lily from room to room.

The child clung to him, probably sensing all was not right. "Mr. Ben, why is the house a mess?"

Ben tried to think of something that would make sense to a child and not frighten her. "Someone must have been playing with things and didn't put them away."

"Where's my mommy?" Lily trembled in his arms and he held on tighter, anger burning below the surface. No child should be afraid to come home.

A quick look around the house, both upstairs and down, confirmed his suspicion. Kate wasn't there and not a single room had been left untouched. Even Lily's room had boxes overturned, clothes flung across the floor and pillows torn open.

By the time he got back to the kitchen, Lily was sobbing quietly. "I want my mommy."

"Tell you what. I bet I know someone who could do with some hugs."

He entered the kitchen and set Lily on the floor.

Pickles barked in his shrill little voice.

Lily ran to the box and lifted the puppy into her arms. "Oh, Pickles." She hugged his neck and held him tight until the puppy squirmed loose and tore out across the floor.

Lily laughed and ran after him into the living room.

Ben followed. Of all the rooms, this one seemed the safest for now. "Stay in the living room, sweetheart. I'll be right back."

He hated leaving the four-year-old alone in the ransacked house, but he didn't know what to expect outside. He jogged to the barn first.

The stalls were empty. He checked the number of saddles in the tack room. All were there and Eddy's truck wasn't in the barnyard. Had Kate gone with Eddy?

Ben couldn't think of a logical reason why she'd leave with Eddy.

Pulse pounding, Ben emerged from the barn and yelled, "Kate! Kate!" He made a complete circle around the barn and scanned the pastures nearby. A few horses trotted over, hoping for a treat. But Ben saw no sign of Kate.

Unwilling to leave Lily alone any longer, he ran toward the house, heart heavy and desperate to find the spitfire redhead. "Kate!"

Moving fast to get back to the house, Ben almost missed the noise coming from the shed.

He ground to a stop and held his breath so that he could hear even the slightest sound.

There it was again. A muffled cry.

"Kate?" He jogged to the shed, careful to limit the crunch of his boots on the gravel.

"Ben! I'm in here," a voice called out, followed by pounding on the wooden door.

Kate.

Ben grabbed the door and yanked. It didn't budge. A latch had been slid home after the door had closed. The wind could have closed the door, but then someone on the outside had to push the bolt through the hasp.

He slid the latch to the side and jerked the door open.

Heat hit him at the same time as Kate's body plowed into his chest.

Her face was red and she wasn't perspiring.

"Holy hell, Kate, how long have you been there?"

"I don't know. It was dark. I must have drifted off. But it seems like forever." She leaned heavily against him and smiled up at him through pale lips. "I could use a drink of water."

He scooped her into his arms. Her skin felt hot and dry. It had to be over a hundred and twenty inside the shed. If she'd been in there for several hours, the saunalike atmosphere could have killed her.

Ben carried Kate toward the house.

"Lily?" Kate's big green eyes gazed up at him.

"She's inside playing with Pickles." Ben's mouth was set in a grim line. "Why did you leave town?"

Kate nestled closer to him, shrugging. "I don't know. I didn't really feel like shopping. I wanted to find out what the key belonged to." She wiggled against him, jammed her hand into her pocket and drew out a small silver flash drive. "I found this."

Ben's eyes widened. "Ah, you found your father's data."

Kate's brows furrowed. "How do you know about it?"

"Hank's team has been busy. I have something for you to watch as soon as we get you hydrated and cooled off."

"I'm fine. Show me."

He shook his head. "Not until I know you're okay."

When they entered the house, Lily ran past, followed by a nipping, barking Pickles. "Hi, Mommy. Someone made a mess and didn't clean up." She stopped in the middle of the floor so fast, Pickles plowed into her. "Why is Mr. Ben carrying you?"

Kate smiled at her daughter, then glanced up at Ben, her brows raised. "Why *are* you carrying me?"

Ben smiled at Lily. "Because I'm big and strong."

Lily giggled and raced off, Pickles nipping at her heels.

Kate moved against him. "You can put me down."

"I will." He glanced at the stairs, then the couch and decided he wouldn't convince her to get in a cool shower. Not when he had news about her father and with Lily playing on the ground floor. Ben laid her on the couch. "Stay."

Kate laughed shakily. "I'm not a dog." Then she looked around the room. "Holy cow."

"Yeah, and it doesn't get better."

Her shoulders sagged. "Will this ever end?"

Her sad expression was almost his undoing. "Sit tight. I'll be back with a tall glass of ice water and a cool rag. But only if you stay."

"I may not be a dog, but I can be bribed." Kate settled back against a tattered throw pillow, her skin cooling in the air-conditioned room.

By the time Ben returned, Kate was shivering, her teeth chattering together so hard she thought they might crack. "I don't know what's wrong with me." Pain stabbed through her calf. She jerked up to a sitting position, grabbed her leg and doubled over. "Ow!"

"What's wrong?" Ben set the ice water on the table.

"Cramp." She tried to rise and fell back against the couch, too dizzy to stand. "I need…to…stretch." She pressed one hand to the cramped muscle, the other to the bridge of her nose.

"Just lay back." Ben pressed her firmly against the cushion, stretched her legs out straight, slid her shoes off her feet and pushed her toes up.

"Ow! Ow! Ow!" Kate reached for his hand, but couldn't quite get there before she fell back against the pillow. Soon, the cramp eased and she lay still, her breathing shallow, the pain gone. "How'd you do that?"

"Works on a charley horse. Figured it would help you with the cramp." He lifted the glass. "Now, let's get some fluids inside you and you'll feel better." He helped her to a sitting position and slid in behind her to hold her up while she drank.

She wanted to drain the glass, but Ben wouldn't let her.

"A little at time. Otherwise you'll just barf it up."

She snorted. "That would be attractive."

"In between sips, you can tell me what happened."

"Before you say anything, I'm sorry." She sipped from the glass, gathering more words as the fuzziness cleared from her head. "I shouldn't have come home by myself."

"Then why did you?"

"I can't rely on you to always be here for me and Lily. I have to be able to handle things on my own."

"When we find out who's behind all the threats. Not a moment sooner."

"I know, I know." Because he was there and she couldn't lie back against the pillows, she let herself lean into the hardness of his muscular chest. "I should have waited for you. And I will from now on." As soon as the words left her mouth, she knew they were a lie. Ben wouldn't be there for her *from now on.* "Or at least until we figure out who's doing this," she added.

"My most immediate concern is getting you hydrated." He pulled her closer and urged her to take another sip.

"Don't worry. I think I could drink a bathtub full of water."

"What happened?"

"I was looking for a lock the key would fit into and had

just found the tackle box in the shed and the flash drive inside it when the door slammed shut. I'd propped the door with a concrete block. Guess it wasn't enough for the gusts of wind."

Ben's arm tightened around her. "It was more than the wind. Someone closed the door on purpose and locked it from the outside."

Kate glanced up, the glass of water forgotten, another tremor shaking her. "Someone locked me in there on purpose? There weren't any windows to let any air in."

Ben's body stiffened beneath hers. "You could have died if we hadn't found you soon enough."

Kate placed the cool glass against her lips, her thoughts on Lily as she plowed through the living room, the puppy chasing after her. "I can't afford to die, Ben. I'm all Lily has," she whispered.

Ben took the glass from her and set it on the table within her reach, then he laid her back on the couch.

She wanted him to hold her longer until the chill of what had almost happened dissipated.

He stood, looking down at her with a frown pulling his brows together. "You're going back to Houston."

Kate tried to push to a sitting position. "Says who?"

"It's not safe here."

"I have nothing left for me in Houston."

"You have Lily."

She started to say something, but bit down on her lip instead. He had a good point. "I can't go back to Houston. It's not any safer. Remember? Someone ransacked my apartment there. I'll bet it has something to do with what's on that flash drive I found."

"You can't tell anyone about it. No one."

"Okay."

"And at least consider leaving here until the dust settles."

She wanted to tell him to quit telling her what to do, but before she could he pressed a finger to her lips.

"I'm not trying to be a jerk. I'm worried about you and Lily. When I came back here and couldn't find you…"

She grasped his hand and held on to it. "I'm glad you did. Mrs. Henderson wasn't due back until tomorrow morning and Eddy could be out until dark working with the cattle. That reminds me."

Ben stared down at her. "Reminds you about what?"

"The CBP was out here investigating the cattle carcasses and asking questions."

Ben's mouth tightened. "Hank says they found a woman's body on the ranch adjacent to the Flying K two weeks ago. She appeared to have been an undocumented alien."

Kate's stomach dropped. "Dead?"

He nodded.

"Wow. I really am in the middle of this, aren't I?" She sat up and waited for the dizziness to clear. "You said you got information off the DVD my father left?"

"We did." He pulled the flash drive from his pocket. "Where's your laptop?"

"It's in a satchel in my bedroom." She sat up and leaned forward, but before she could rise, Ben pressed a hand to her shoulder.

"I'll get it." Ben collected the laptop from her bedroom and returned to the living room where he booted up the system and plugged in the flash drive. "Have you had lunch?"

"No. Marge said she left a pie on the counter and to help yourself." She didn't glance his way, her eyes trained on the screen. When it came up with her father's image she drew in a sharp breath, her heart squeezing so tightly she was afraid it would stop. "That's him? That's my father?"

Chapter Fifteen

Ben entered the kitchen, the sound of the video barely reaching him. He figured he'd chosen the coward's way out by ducking into the kitchen while Kate reviewed her father's first and last words to her. Ben tried to block the words from his mind and Kate's reaction by keeping busy.

As he glanced around, he noted that the back door swung wide open on its hinges, the hot Texas wind blowing into the house. The countertop was empty, no pie there, only a few crumbs. Perhaps Kate had been mistaken. The pantry door also hung open. When Ben peered inside, he noted cans lying sideways on the shelves and strewn across the floor. Someone had been in a hurry to get in and get out of the kitchen. Another unauthorized entry. Since the front door most likely hadn't been locked when Kate left the house to look into the shed and barn, it wasn't a forced entry, but an entry nonetheless. The other break-ins had been just that. The doors had been locked. Whoever had come in hadn't broken a window. He'd used a key or jimmied the lock.

Could it have been the same person responsible for locking Kate in the shed? Ben had stopped by the hardware store and picked up all new doorknobs and keys for the house. He'd gotten enough copies to give Mrs. H. one and one for himself and Kate.

Maybe changing the locks in the house would keep Kate and Lily safer.

God, he hoped so.

Ben quickly made a sandwich out of bread, leftover slices of the ham Mrs. H. had cooked for breakfast and a dab of mustard. Ben didn't know if Kate liked mustard, but he added it anyway. There was a lot he didn't know about Kate.

If he was smart, he'd keep it that way. He couldn't afford to get attached.

His stomach roiled every time he thought of Kate locked in the hotbox of a shed. If he hadn't come when he had...

He wrapped the sandwich in a paper towel, grabbed a bag of chips and hurried back into the living room, bracing himself for the storm of emotions Kate might be experiencing and another chance to hold her in his arms.

Lily had crawled up on the couch with her mother and lay with her head in Kate's lap. The four-year-old's silky, light golden-red hair curled around her face, one hand tucked beneath her cheek. She was fast asleep, petal-pink lips parted.

Kate stared down at her daughter, smoothing her hand across her hair. Every so often, she'd brush a tear from her eye before it fell onto Lily.

Ben froze on the threshold of the room, holding the sandwich and bag of chips, his chest hurting so badly he held his breath to keep the pain from spreading.

Kate blinked and she looked up at him, her green eyes darker than the deepest forest. "My father was a drug runner."

"Yes, but he wised up and went to work for the good guys."

She looked up at him, tears welling in her eyes. "He didn't abandon us."

"No. He didn't. He sent you away to keep you safe."

A single fat tear slipped down her cheek.

Another blow to Ben's insides, tearing away at the wall

he'd constructed against ever falling in love with a woman or a child again.

"I wish..." Kate started, glanced down at her hand and then up at him. "I wish you'd give me that sandwich."

Ben almost laughed. She had been about to say something else, but settled for focusing on something she could control. A sandwich. A lousy ham-and-mustard sandwich.

Kate held out her hand.

Ben shook himself out of the trance and handed it to her. When their fingers touched, Kate flinched, her eyes widening. With her other hand, she twined hers around his, dragging him closer.

He leaned over her, his gaze capturing her green one.

When he was within kissing range, she stopped. "Thank you for being here for us." Then she kissed him, her hand circling behind his neck.

Barely aware of where they were, the child in Kate's lap and the near-death experience, Ben kissed her back, his lips caressing, his tongue sweeping across hers.

Lily stirred and sighed.

Ben broke it off, his lips thinning. "You don't have to kiss me to thank me. I'm just doing my job."

"Well, you're doing a darned good job, then." She tipped her chin up. "And I *wanted* to kiss you, not as payment for saving my life, although I do appreciate that you did. Thank you for helping me learn more about my father. I wish I'd had a chance to know him."

"Based on the video, he wished the same." Ben swallowed the hard knot forming in his throat. "Want me to carry her up the stairs?"

"Please." Kate brushed Lily's hair back from her forehead and pressed a kiss to her temple, then leaned back so that Ben could take Lily from her lap.

Ben lifted the child and headed up the stairs, still reeling from the kiss, more bothered by it than by having made love to her the night before.

The woman trusted him to keep her safe. What scared him most was that he didn't know who to keep her safe from.

Kate followed. "I'm going for a shower, unless you want to go first?"

"You go. I need to make a couple phone calls." He tucked Lily into bed and headed down the stairs, anxious to talk with Jenkins and Hank. When he heard the water come on in the shower, he lifted the phone from the receiver and punched the numbers for his buddy back in the Austin Police Department. A quick glance at the clock indicated the hour was late, but not too late to call Jenkins. He owed him.

"Hello."

Ben recognized the gravelly voice on the other end of the connection. "Harding here. What did you find?"

"Ben? Didn't you get my message?" The gravel left Jenkins's voice.

"No. Reception stinks out here. Give me what you have."

"Masters searched through Rolando Gonzalez's phone records. He's got a cousin he calls pretty often in your area. A José Mendez. I have an address they pulled up based on the phone number. Here."

Ben jotted the address on a notepad and ripped off the page, stuffing it in his pocket. "Any other reason Mendez could be considered a person of interest?"

"He happens to own a commercial driver's license. He drives the big trucks."

"Something big enough to transport people and drugs?"

"Yeah. Since he's in your neighborhood, I suggest you check him out. See what other connections he has."

"Will do." He'd notify Hank and let him track it down.

"Look, Jenkins, I need you to dig into anyone and everyone these guys may have had contact with."

"Hey, information flow goes both ways, you know. What do you know that I don't?"

"They are smuggling women and girls up from Mexico through here. We encountered a couple pickup truckloads last night."

"You called the Customs and Border Protection?"

"Yeah, by the time they got the choppers up, the trucks had disappeared. We need to find them before they are sold or killed."

"I'll get right on it." Jenkins paused. "Oh, and one other thing. That Robert Sanders you had me look up?"

"Yeah, what about him?"

"He was a friend of Frank Davis. Spent time up here in Austin going to social functions. The society pages have photos of them drinking together."

Ben's heart squeezed tight. "Thanks. I'll check into Sanders."

"And Harding," Jenkins began, then paused. "Be careful. The Mexican Mafia can be brutal on both sides of the border."

Ben hung up and glanced at the top of the stairs.

The door to Kate's room opened and she stepped out, wrapped in a soft pink robe, her hair up in a towel turban. Her brows dipped. "Who was on the phone?"

"I made a call to a friend of mine who has connections with the Austin Police Department."

"Why Austin?"

"I might be grasping at straws. But I hope to find something useful that will help me keep you safe and help those women."

"You'll tell me what you find, won't you?"

"You bet," Ben lied. "Want me to check your room?"

Kate stood at the doorway to her bedroom. "No. I can do it myself."

"I don't mind and I'd feel better knowing it's safe." Ben

climbed the stairs, brushed her aside and entered, checking beneath the bed, pulling back the covers and sheets and
opening the closet. "All clear. No snakes."

She gave him a shaky smile and touched his arm as he
passed her. "Thanks."

Ben had to get away before he was tempted to kiss her
again. He really wanted to and that would solve nothing and
complicate everything even more.

As he descended to the first floor, a shadow passed by
the front window.

If he hadn't been looking that way at that exact moment,
Ben would have missed it. He focused on the window next
to it and the shadow appeared again.

Ben's pulse leaped. He turned out the light in the hallway,
lifted his Glock from where he'd left it on top of a bookshelf
and slipped out the back door, rounding the house from the
opposite direction.

As he eased his way around the side, he ducked low, careful to tread lightly and stop to listen every few steps.

When he rounded the corner near the kitchen side of the
house, he paused behind a rosebush and waited, his ears
cocked toward the front of the house.

A twig snapped close by.

Ben held the Glock in front of him and peered around
the bush.

A dark figure hovered in the shadows by the kitchen door.
He wasn't very tall, but he was barrel-chested and stocky.

Ben inched forward to a better position. If the man tried
to make a run for it, Ben could head him off.

When a shadowy hand reached for the doorknob, Ben
stood, pointed the gun at the man's back and said, "Don't
move if you want to live. I have a gun trained on you."

The man froze.

For a moment Ben thought he'd listened, then in a burst
of movement, the shadow spun and ran.

Even as he shouted, "Stop, or I'll shoot," Ben gave chase, pounding the ground behind the darkly clothed man. He could have just fired off a round and probably hit the assailant, but Ben didn't want to kill the man. He wanted answers and this guy might have some.

The intruder headed for the barn, running hell-for-leather, but he was no match for Ben, who'd been running all his life and kept in good shape.

Before the stranger disappeared around the corner, Ben threw himself at the man's legs, catching enough of a pant leg to bring the man down.

They crashed into the hard-packed dirt.

Ben leaped to his feet, pushed a foot into the middle of the man's back and pointed the gun at his head. "Don't even think about moving." With his spare hand, Ben grabbed the man's arm and pulled it up behind his back. "Get up."

The guy stood. "Let me go, please. I didn't steal anything but food. I'll pay it back, I promise."

Ben pushed the man's arm up to the middle of his back. "To the house."

"I can't. If they see me, they'll kill me."

"Who will?"

"I can't say. I know too much." The man twisted. "If they know I'm here…if I'm caught…I'm as good as dead. Please, let me go."

Ben struggled to maintain his hold on the desperate man. "Slow down. No one's going to hurt you unless you try to get away from me." Ben lifted the arm higher and shoved the man toward the back door to the house. "In the house. Now."

"Ben?" The kitchen porch light blinked on and Kate stepped out, her bathrobe wrapped tightly around her body. "Ben?"

"I'm here." He eased the man forward.

Kate's mouth dropped open for a second, then she closed it and ran forward. "What can I do to help?"

"Take the gun and hold it on him."

Kate took the weapon from Ben and held it with both hands, pointing the barrel at the stranger's head. "Who is he?" she asked.

"I haven't gotten that far." Ben pushed the man forward. "Answer the lady."

"Larry," he said, his head down. "Larry Sites."

"The man who disappeared the day my father died?" She stopped, her eyes widening in the light from the porch. "Were you there when he died?"

"Yes, ma'am," the man answered softly.

Kate jumped in front of him, her mouth set in a tight line. "Was it really natural causes? Or did you kill him?"

Sites stood still, his gaze never wavering from Kate's. "He was murdered. But I didn't do it."

Kate gasped, her hands shaking, the gun tipping wildly. "Who did?"

"Can we take this into the house?" His head swiveled from right to left, his eyes wide, scared. "I'm a sitting duck out here."

"Kate, honey, get inside." Ben glanced around the barnyard.

"You can let go of my arm. I'm not going to run. I'm tired of hiding." Sites sighed. "I might as well be dead."

Kate stepped up onto the porch and opened the kitchen door. "If you didn't do it, who killed my father?"

"I didn't have any beef with Kyle Kendrick. I just happened to be around when he was killed."

"Why didn't you tell anyone who did it?" Ben pushed him closer to the house.

"No one would have believed me, not when it was—" A loud pop sounded and Larry's body jerked so hard he pulled free of Ben's hold.

"Kate, get down!" Ben dropped to the ground.

Kate threw herself into the house.

After a long minute, Ben whispered loud enough to be heard in the house, "Kate? Are you okay?"

"I'm fine. What happened?"

Ben inched forward to where Larry Sites lay on the ground. His hand encountered warm sticky liquid and his chest tightened. "Someone shot Sites."

"Is he…"

Ben found the man's throat and felt for a pulse. Nothing.

"He's dead." Ben crawled over the body and made a run for the door.

Kate stepped aside as he entered and slammed the door behind him. "What just happened?"

"Sites is dead. Someone shot him."

Kate pressed a hand to her chest. "I'll call the sheriff."

She hurried to where the phone sat on the table in the hallway. When she lifted the receiver, her hand shook so much she dropped it.

Ben caught the handset. "Let me." He held the device to his ear only to discover there was no dial tone. "It's not working."

Kate's brows furrowed. "It was working a few minutes ago."

"Either the phone system is down or someone cut your line."

She wrapped her arms around herself. "I don't like this. I should check on Lily."

"Do that, and get her ready to leave."

"Where are we going?" She gathered the edges of her robe closer, her body trembling.

Ben pulled her into his arms and pressed a kiss to her forehead. "I don't know, but we're not staying here. Now go. Stay away from the windows and don't turn on any lights. We don't know if the shooter is still out there." He turned and would have walked away, but Kate's hand on his arm stopped him.

"Where are you going?" she asked.

"To check outside and see what I can find."

Her fingers tightened on his arm. "Don't go."

"I'll be okay. Lock the door behind me and hold on to this." He reached up to the top of the shelf where he'd left her loaded Glock and handed it to her, checking that the safety was on. "You know how to use it. Point, click the safety off and shoot. Just make sure it's not me. I'll call out when I want back in. Otherwise leave all the doors locked. If you have to…leave them locked until morning when Mrs. H. arrives." He kissed her lips this time. He couldn't resist. She looked so vulnerable in her pale pink robe. "Relax. I'll be all right."

Her hand trembled as she cupped his jaw. "What if you don't come back?"

"I will." He kissed her again, this time his tongue pushing past her teeth to slide along hers. It was a lot harder this time to break away, but he did. He needed to know if the shooter was still out there. If he was and he planned to target Ben and Kate, they were pretty much trapped inside the house.

Kate followed him to the back door. When Ben slipped out, she closed the door behind him and locked it, her heartbeat pounding against her rib cage. "Please be okay," she whispered. Then she turned and hurried up the stairs to get ready for whatever happened next.

Fumbling around in the dark, her pulse racing, Kate dressed and grabbed a bag out of her closet. She shoved in a change of clothes for herself, her brush and toothbrush.

In Lily's room, she gathered an outfit, shoes and Lily's favorite doll, shoving them all into the bag and zipping it closed.

Pickles stood, stretched, then leaned up against the side of the box and whined.

Afraid he'd wake Lily, Kate lifted him from the box and cuddled him beneath her chin, inhaling the warm sweet scent of puppy and drawing comfort from the creature. "It's going to be okay. Ben will be back and we'll all be fine."

The minutes stretched by. Kate set the puppy in the box, looped the bag over her shoulder and carried it down the stairs, placing it by the front door. She returned to Lily's room and carried the box with Pickles down the steps. On her last trip, she carried Lily down and laid her on the love seat out of view of the windows. Her little girl barely stirred throughout the process.

Sounds of an engine drew Kate to the living room window. She peeked around the edges, careful not to provide too much of a silhouette should a shooter decide to fire at her.

Ben's truck pulled up right in front of the porch and stopped, the lights glaring out into the side yard. Ben dropped out of the driver's seat and rounded the front of the truck, leaping up onto the porch.

Kate was there, unlocking the door even as he knocked.

He burst through and closed the door behind him.

"Did you see anything?"

"Nothing. I found fresh motorcycle tracks, but whoever rode in on it was gone. Ready?"

Kate nodded. "What about Sites?"

"There's nothing we can do for him but report the murder. We have to get you somewhere safe first. Then we can notify the police."

Ben lifted Lily from the love seat and cradled her in his arms.

Kate slung the bag and her purse over her shoulder and hefted the box with the puppy.

Ben's brows dipped. "You have all that?"

She smiled. "I'm a mother."

"Okay, straight out. I'm right behind you."

Kate sucked in a deep breath and let it out. It did nothing to calm her nerves, but she stepped out onto the porch and down to the pickup, sliding the box onto one side of the backseat floorboard. She tossed the overnight bag onto the other side and climbed into the passenger seat, sitting low.

Ben came out half a minute later, carrying Lily. He settled her into her booster seat, tightened her straps and fumbled with the box containing the puppy. Finally, Ben climbed into the driver's side and shifted into Drive.

Before he'd gone ten feet down the driveway, headlights flashed on directly in front of them and the red and blue of a law enforcement vehicle whirled like circus lights.

Ben had to stop or risk running into the vehicle.

"It's the sheriff." Kate reached for her door handle. "We can tell him about Sites and the shooter."

Ben grabbed her arm. "Stay put and don't say anything."

"Why?"

"Trust me."

"Please step out of the vehicle," Sheriff Fulmer called out, service weapon drawn. He approached the driver's side of the truck while Deputy Schillinger came up on Kate's side.

"Sheriff, what's this about?"

"We had a report of gunshots fired. Please step out of the vehicle and keep your hands where I can see them."

Ben got out slowly, his hands held high. "Your report was correct. Someone shot Larry Sites. His body is lying on the ground outside the kitchen door."

To Ben, his gaze narrowed. "Cool your heels, cowboy."

The sheriff nodded toward Ben, his gun trained on Ben's chest. "Up against the truck and spread your legs."

Kate could barely breathe as she slid down out of the truck. "You're worrying about the wrong man. Whoever shot Sites might still be out there."

Schillinger jerked his gun toward Ben. "Look out, sheriff, he's got a gun."

Kate stepped in front of the deputy's weapon. "He's licensed to carry one."

"But he's not licensed to kill." The sheriff nodded to the deputy. "Check it out."

Sheriff Fulmer removed the Glock from Ben's waistband and tucked it into his belt. While the deputy rounded the house to the kitchen, the sheriff patted Ben down, running his hands up Ben's legs and into his pockets, emptying them of their contents. He opened Ben's wallet and checked the driver's license. "Says he's Ben Harding from Austin." Fulmer tossed the wallet onto the hood of the truck and continued his search. When he delved into Ben's front pocket, he pulled out a small silver flash drive and held it up to the light. His hand closed around the tiny device and he slid it into his pocket.

Kate leaned forward. "Hey, that's not yours."

"And you're wrong." The sheriff continued to search Ben's other pocket. "It's evidence."

"It's mine," Kate said. "You have no right to take it."

"It's on a man who might have committed a murder."

"He didn't!"

"Leave it, Kate," Ben warned her. "We'll get it back when we clear up this mess."

Two minutes later, Deputy Schillinger returned. "It's Sites, all right, and he's dead as a doornail. Gunshot wound."

Kate bit down on her lip, wanting to say more, to stop what was happening to Ben and get back the data storage device her father had placed in her possession.

Sheriff Fulmer grabbed Ben's wrist and pulled it behind him, then the other and zip-tied them together at the base of his spine.

"Am I being arrested?" Ben stood tall. "I know my rights."

"You're being arrested on suspicion of a homicide. You have the right to remain silent and I suggest you do and get into the car." Fulmer shoved Ben toward the sheriff's vehicle.

"Sites tried to break in and when I stopped him, someone shot him."

Kate stepped forward. "Ben didn't kill Sites. Someone else did."

Schillinger waved his gun in her face. "Don't get in the way or you'll be going with him. In which case, we'd have to place your little girl in the care of child welfare services."

As the sheriff pushed Ben into the car, Ben called over his shoulder, "Kate, get Lily to somewhere safe."

Kate's shoulders sagged, her eyes filling with tears. The only person she'd felt safe with was being hauled off in a police car. "Where?"

"Ma'am." Deputy Schillinger stepped between Kate and Ben. "I suggest you climb into the truck and drive into town in front of us. You can't stay here, since this is now officially a crime scene."

"But Ben didn't do it," Kate insisted.

The sheriff stopped in front of her. "Are you admitting to the crimes?"

"No, of course not." Kate's head spun, her vision clouding. What the hell was going on? Had the entire world turned upside down?

"Kate," Ben called out. "Go to town. Get help, call a lawyer, just don't argue with them."

"For a murderer, he gives good advice." Schillinger gripped her elbow, dragged her around the truck and shoved her up into the driver's seat. "Drive."

With no other choice and Lily to consider, Kate did what she was told and drove into town, the rotating lights from the sheriff's vehicle filling her rearview mirror.

She held on to her sanity, her resolve strengthening as she reached the city limits. First stop for her was Cara Jo's Diner where she hoped Cara Jo was home above the restaurant and had a phone she could use. She had to get in touch with Hank.

Chapter Sixteen

Ben leaned over the backseat, his gaze on the taillights of his truck as Kate turned left into the diner parking lot. Good, she was going to her only friend in town, Cara Jo, where she could use a phone and contact Hank with the number he'd given her earlier. Hank would help clear up this mess and send reinforcements to protect her and Lily.

Ben could kick himself for not getting Kate to safety faster. He swiveled in his seat as the sheriff's SUV passed the diner and continued on to the sheriff's office. "If you'll look at the gun, you'll note that it hasn't been discharged."

Sheriff Fulmer ignored him, pulling to the side of the road a block away from the diner. "Schillinger, you're to stay here and keep an eye on Ms. Langsdon."

"Why?" Schillinger asked. "I thought we had our killer."

Fulmer glared at him and said in a deadly tone, "Get out."

Schillinger muttered beneath his breath as he climbed out of the SUV.

The sheriff shot down the road, sliding into the parking lot at the sheriff's station. He got out and left Ben in the backseat as he unlocked the door to the office. Apparently the offices were only open during the day.

Ben waited for the sheriff to come back and lead him into a jail cell.

Fulmer didn't even glance back at the SUV as he entered the office and closed the door behind him.

After a few minutes, Ben frowned, working the zip tie around his wrists, trying to free his hands. Unfortunately, the sheriff had cinched it good and most likely the back doors of the SUV were locked from the driver's control panel. Even if he got the zip tie off his wrists, he'd have to break the window or cage separating the passenger from the driver. Why would the sheriff leave a murder suspect sitting in the back of a vehicle?

A moment later the sheriff stormed out of the office, flinging the door so hard it cracked against the wall. "Where is it?" he yelled, his face red, his eyes round, angry and maniacal. Fulmer yanked open the back door of the SUV, grabbed Ben by the front of his shirt, hauled him out and slammed him against the vehicle. "Where the hell is it?"

"I don't know what you're talking about."

"The database. The information Kendrick left to his daughter. Where is it? And don't tell me you don't know. You spoke to Derringer on the telephone and said you had a flash drive." He shook Ben and flung him against the SUV again.

Without his hands to balance, Ben tripped and fell to the ground.

Fulmer kicked him in the side. "Tell me!"

Pain shot through his side where the sheriff's boot crashed into his ribs. When the sheriff pulled his leg back to deliver another kick, Ben rolled to the side to avoid it. "Why? What's on it that you'd accuse me of a murder I didn't commit?"

"I need that damned data. My wife's life depends on it." Fulmer reached down and dragged Ben to his feet. "Please, tell me. Tell me where it is."

Ben shook his head. "I don't have it."

"Sheriff," a voice called out. "Sheriff!" Deputy Schillinger ran toward them, sweating, red-faced and breathing erratically.

"I thought I told you to watch the girl."

"She went into the diner...with the kid." Schillinger dragged in a deep breath. "Then she left the diner." The deputy doubled over, wheezing. "I couldn't...follow her... without a vehicle."

"Damn! Which way did she go?"

"West on Main."

The sheriff held Ben by the collar of his shirt. "If she has it, I'll get it. If she doesn't, you'll get it for me before you get your precious fiancée back." He slung Ben away from the SUV. "Don't let him out of your sight."

Fulmer climbed into his vehicle and spun the vehicle around, burning a trail of rubber against the pavement.

His heart racing, Ben's gaze followed the sheriff. "What did he mean, his wife's life depends on that data?" Ben asked the deputy.

"I shouldn't be saying this, but the best I can tell, the drug cartel kidnapped her when she went down to visit her family in Monterrey, Mexico." Deputy Schillinger hooked his hand through Ben's elbow and started toward the sheriff's office.

Ben dug his heels into the pavement. "Why didn't he call for help?"

"They threatened to kill her if he told anyone." The deputy tugged on his arm. "Come on. I've got a cell with your name on it." He led him toward the building.

Ben went along with him, every escape scenario he could imagine racing through his head.

When Schillinger dropped his hold on Ben's elbow and reached for the doorknob, Ben stepped back. "I'm sorry, but I can't go with you." Ben ducked his head and rammed into the deputy's back, sending him flying headfirst into the metal door.

He hit with a sickening thud and crumpled to the ground.

With no time to spare, Ben ran back toward the diner, his wrists still bound together.

When he reached the restaurant, he raced around back and kicked the door until Cara Jo peeked out the window, then threw open the door and came out on the landing above him. "Ben? Oh, thank God." Wearing a robe and flip-flops, she rushed down the stairs.

Ben's heart squeezed in his chest and his rib ached where the sheriff had kicked him. "Where's Kate?"

"She brought Lily and the puppy inside, then went back out for her overnight bag. Next thing I know she's driving off without telling me where she went."

Cara Jo pressed her hands to her cheeks. "From what I could see, there was a man in the passenger seat."

"Who was it?"

"I don't know. All I saw was his silhouette as the truck sped out of the parking lot. I called 911 and the dispatcher said she'd get word to the sheriff."

Ben gripped Cara Jo's hand. "Where's Lily?"

"She and Pickles are sleeping in my bed upstairs."

"I need a phone."

"Come up and use mine."

Ben pushed ahead of Cara Jo and raced up the stairs. The living quarters above the diner were small but decorated tastefully. "Where?"

"By the kitchen counter." Cara Jo pointed to the telephone. "You're not going to be able to do much with your hands tied behind your back." The diner owner pulled a butcher knife out of a drawer and sliced through the zip tie.

Ben rubbed his raw wrists for a second to get the feeling back into his fingertips, then dialed Hank.

The man answered on the first ring. "Derringer speaking."

"It's Ben. I need help, ASAP. Someone has Kate and I don't know who it is or where they're going."

"Slow down and tell me what happened."

Ben gave his boss the abbreviated version of what he'd

learned that day. "Someone wants that data file and they're willing to kill to get it."

"Does Kate have it?"

"No."

"They'll use her as leverage to get you to give it to them."

"I figured that." Ben leaned his head against the wall. "The sheriff was with me when someone else took Kate. Larry Sites is dead and I have no idea where to start looking for Kate."

"Ben, hold on." Sounds of keyboard clicks echoed across the phone, then Hank was back. "I had a tracking device placed on your truck. If she's in it, we can find her. I have my IT guy pulling it up as we speak."

"Thank God." Ben sagged against the counter. "Hey, this might be small, but my guy in Austin said Robert Sanders was photographed at a fund-raising event in Austin with Frank Davis."

"The man you killed?"

Ben winced. "Yeah. Did you find anything else about Sanders? He approached Kate the other day, claiming to be a friend of her father's, which doesn't make sense since most people around here claim Kate's father kept to himself. He didn't have friends, just acquaintances."

"From what I'd known of Kyle Kendrick, he didn't talk much to anyone and was always on the road, traveling from here to Mexico and back."

"You think Sanders could be the U.S. link between Mexico and the human trafficking?"

"Could be. Be careful. If he is, he has a lot to lose and he'd gladly take down anyone who gets in the way of his enterprise." Keyboard clicks sounded on Hank's side. "My IT guy says the truck's headed out County Road 949. From what we can see on the satellite map, there's not much out there but a diesel mechanic shop and some storage buildings."

Ben's hand froze on the receiver. "Would the address of the mechanic's shop be 1421 Highway 949 West?"

"Looks like it. Why?"

"My Austin contact said the man who supplied Frank the woman he killed had a cousin who lives at that address."

"Ben, I'm calling in the Border Protection and Texas Rangers. Don't try to go in there without backup. You could be stirring up a rattlesnake's den."

"Hank, they have Kate. She was my responsibility."

"Ben!" Hank shouted.

Ben hung up and sprinted for the door.

Cara Jo stood there dangling a set of keys. "You can't get there without a vehicle. Take my Mustang and bring Kate back safe."

"Lily?"

"I'll take good care of her."

"Do you have a gun?"

"I do and I know how to use it." She lifted a 9 mm Beretta from a shelf in an antique cabinet. "Girl can't be too careful when she lives alone."

"Don't let anyone in. Not anyone until I get back here with Kate. As a matter of fact, hit Redial and get Hank to send someone out to stand guard."

"Will do." She shoved him out the door. "Now go. I want my new friend back. Alive. Oh, and there's another one of these—" she waved her gun "—under the driver's seat and it's loaded."

Ben ran to the bottom of the stairs and leaped into a vintage 1967 Mustang. Seconds later he'd skidded out on Main Street and turned onto County Road 949 headed west, having flashbacks of when he'd gotten home too late to save Julia and Sarah. History could not repeat itself. He wouldn't let it.

His hands tightened around the steering wheel and he

jammed the accelerator to the floor. The car was old, but it packed a lot of power. He hoped it was enough to get him there in time.

"You never were my father's friend, were you?" Kate stared straight ahead, her hands clutching the steering wheel, thankful she'd unloaded Lily and the puppy first before she'd come back down to the truck for her overnight bag. At least they were safe from this latest threat. She risked a quick glance at the man beside her.

Robert Sanders sat in the passenger seat with a pistol pointed at her side. "We were business partners. He helped me find the drugs in Mexico and I sold them."

Kate's heart sank into her gut. The fact the man was admitting all this to her was a sure sign he planned to kill her when all was said and done.

Tears threatened, but Kate wouldn't let them fall. She didn't plan on dying today. Lily needed a parent to raise her. She'd already lost one. Kate would be damned if she lost another.

"I'll ask you again. Where is the flash drive your father left you?"

"I told you. The sheriff took it from Ben when he arrested him for murder."

"Then you'd better hope the sheriff doesn't decrypt the data before your fiancé gets it back."

"I suppose the information on that thumb drive implicates you in the human and drug trafficking going on around here."

"Amongst others who'd rather not be named."

"What are you going to do with me?"

Before they got too far out of town, Sanders punched buttons on his cell phone one-handed and hit Send. "I have Kendrick's daughter and I know you have the thumb drive. If you don't want your wife to die, you'll meet me at the shop, immediately." Sanders paused. "Ten minutes. Be there or I make the call."

Kate shot a glance at Sanders. "I'm not Ben's wife."

"I wasn't talking to Ben." He slipped his cell phone into his shirt pocket and steadied the gun on Kate. "Faster."

Kate eased her foot onto the accelerator. Sanders had called her on her ploy to slow down enough for someone to catch up. The farther away from town, the less likely Ben would find her.

Although how he'd get free from jail, she didn't have a clue. She hadn't even had a chance to call Hank and let him know what was going on. When Cara Jo discovered her missing, she'd call the police. A lot of good that would do.

After what felt like a very long time, Sanders leaned forward. "Turn left at the next driveway."

Kate slowed as the headlights from Ben's pickup reflected off several large metal buildings and an old barn.

"Stop."

Kate slammed her foot on the brakes.

Sanders shot forward, hitting his head on the dash. "Damn you, woman. You should have left when Snake warned you."

"My father left me that ranch. I wasn't going anywhere." Kate shifted into Park.

"You're going to wish you had." Sanders grabbed her by the hair and dragged her out of the truck through the passenger side, tossing her to the ground. "Get up. And don't try anything. I'd just as soon kill you as look at you. You Kendricks have been nothing but a thorn in my side."

He kicked her in the ribs.

Pain radiated through her rib cage as Kate staggered to her feet, reluctant to stay down where the man could kick her again.

A man with a bandanna and a tattoo on his arm stepped out of the shadows. *"Buenas noches, Patrón."*

"Did Sites spill the truth before you shot him?"

"No, amigo."

"I asked you to take care of him weeks ago."

"He was a slippery one."

"Where are the other men?"

"Moving the first shipment. They will be gone all night."

Sanders pushed Kate toward the man. "Put her with the others."

"Con las putas?"

"Sí. Do as I said."

The man with the snake tattoo grabbed Kate's arm and hustled her toward the derelict barn.

Before they'd gone two yards, headlights swung into the driveway.

Guillermo stopped and stared back toward the road.

Kate tried to wiggle out of his grip, but his fingers tightened on her arm.

Sanders held his pistol out and waved it. "Get out of the car, Sheriff."

The sheriff remained inside.

Sanders shot out a headlight and held up his cell phone. "I'm dialing now. Your wife is as good as dead."

Fulmer climbed out of the SUV with his hands raised. "Don't. Delia is all I have. Don't hurt her."

"If you didn't want me to hurt her, why were you snooping around the Flying K?" Sanders asked.

"I'd heard Kendrick had a flash drive full of the names of the people he'd been working with on both sides of the border."

"Heard? As in, bugged the phone?"

The sheriff shrugged. "I figured Kendrick's daughter might have learned something from her father."

"Her father is dead and we'd been all over the house and found nothing. Even in his computer."

"It didn't hurt to be aware, so I bugged the phone." The sheriff took a step closer. "When I heard Harding talking about a flash drive, I knew you wouldn't want it to get into the wrong hands."

"Wrong like yours?" Sanders held out his hand. "Give it to me."

The sheriff pulled out his pockets. "I don't have it."

"Kate here tells me you picked it off her fiancé."

"I confiscated a flash drive but it wasn't the right one. It didn't contain the data, only a video message from Kendrick to his daughter telling her of the drive and where to find it."

"You lie!" Sanders shot at Fulmer's feet.

Kate flinched.

The tattooed man seemed as reluctant as Kate to leave the little scene unfolding.

"I wouldn't risk my wife's life over a data device. I want her back. Alive."

Sanders shook his head. "You're a stupid fool. Your wife doesn't *want* to come back."

Fulmer's face blanched. "What do you mean?"

"She left you and returned to her family."

"She went back for vacation. Someone kidnapped her. Her parents were beside themselves when they told me."

"They told you what she wanted them to tell you. She's been working for me on the other side of the border making good money sending me the goods."

"No." Sheriff Fulmer backed away a step. "She wouldn't do that to me. Delia loves me."

"She loves money more." Sanders's lips twitched. "And the beauty of it is, you've been working for me to keep her safe. Ironic, don't you think?"

"You bastard!" Sheriff Fulmer lunged at Sanders.

A shot rang out as Fulmer reached Sanders.

The two men staggered, the sheriff falling to the ground, a hand clutched to his chest.

Kate dived for the man, but came up short when her captor jerked her backward.

Blood dribbled from the side of the sheriff's mouth and he stared up at the night sky. "I loved her...."

Kate choked back a sob. The man had to have loved his wife very much to have risked his career and his life to save her.

Her thoughts turned to Ben. If something were to happen to her, he'd blame himself for failing to reach her in time. She refused to be the next victim on his watch. Ben deserved a chance to love again. He was a good man and he'd be a good husband and father again, if only he could believe in himself.

"Guillermo!" Sanders jerked his head toward the barn. "Get her inside and burn the building."

As the tattooed man dragged her away, Kate prayed she'd live long enough to tell Ben...

Tell him what?

That she loved him? After knowing him such a short time? Could it be love? Her father said he'd fallen in love with her mother the moment he met her. Could it have been the same for her?

Love or not, she wanted the chance to get to know Ben better, to see if what she felt for him was love. She'd never thought she'd love another after losing Troy. But Ben...he could be her second chance. Her heart was big enough to love again.

Guillermo unlocked a padlock securing a heavy chain to the door of the barn and pulled the chain through the handles. Before he could shove her in, she backed up sharply and jerked out of his grip, then plowed into his side, sending him sailing through the open doorway. Several female, frightened cries erupted from within.

"Mierda!" the big man shouted.

Before Guillermo could regain his balance, Kate ran for the shadows.

A shot rang out, spitting dust up beside her, but she made

it to where the moonlight cast a deep shadow next to the big old barn.

"Get her!" Sanders shouted.

Footsteps pounded on the gravel behind her.

Her pulse banging against her eardrums, Kate ran as fast as she could, tripping over objects hidden in the dark. When she cleared the back of the building, a wide-open field loomed in front of her, illuminated by the moon.

If she stepped away from the barn, she'd be found. If she stayed where she was, she'd be caught.

The whirring of a helicopter sounded in the distance and a long beam of light moved toward the barn and building complex.

It had to be the cavalry. Kate dropped to her knees and choked back a sob. Ben must have escaped.

An arm circled her neck and yanked her up.

Kate cried out, struggling to get her feet beneath her.

Headlights blasted into the compound and sirens blared in the distance.

Guillermo hauled Kate out into the open and shoved her toward his boss. He flipped a switchblade out, the smooth metal glinting in the beams of the car's headlights.

Sanders grabbed her hair and jammed the gun into her cheek. "Move and I kill her."

"Don't hurt her." Ben's voice washed over Kate like a cool balm in a blazing desert. He climbed out of an older model Mustang, carrying a gun aimed at Sanders. "I have what you're looking for."

He was there. Ben had come, against all odds.

"You give me Kate. I'll give you the device." Ben reached into his pocket with his left hand.

"Why don't I just shoot you and get the device myself?"

"You could do that, but then you might not have time to find it and destroy it before that helicopter arrives, and what would your friends on both sides of the border do to someone who let that kind of information get out?" Ben tipped his head toward the sky. "You only have a few seconds."

"Put your gun down," Sanders demanded.

Ben didn't budge.

"Do it—" Sanders shoved Kate in front of him "—or I put a bullet through her pretty head."

BEN SUCKED IN a breath and let it out slowly, praying for the right move, the right decision, the one that ended with Kate going home to Lily and raising her daughter in peace.

"Don't, Ben." Kate's voice shook. "He's going to kill me anyway. And you, too."

"Shut up." Sanders jerked her hair back hard.

Kate whimpered but didn't cry. "No," she said. "You shut up." In a flurry of movement, Kate slammed her elbow into Sanders's gut and dived for the dirt.

A shot rang at the same time Ben fired, clipping Sanders in the shoulder.

Sanders staggered backward into Guillermo, knocking the other man to the ground. When Sanders rolled over and staggered to his feet, clutching at his belly, Ben was there, his gun drawn, ready to kill the man.

Overhead, the helicopter moved into position, a spotlight filling the yard with blinding light.

Ben held his gun steady. He bent to touch Kate's shoulder. Her face was down in the dirt, but he felt for a pulse. After a second or two a strong, rhythmic thump beat against his fingers and he let the air he'd been holding out of his lungs.

Cars with rotating blue and red lights and sirens screaming whipped into the yard.

Kate stirred, then sat up with a jerk. "Ben!"

"I'm here."

"Oh, thank God." She threw herself into his arms and hugged him so tight she almost knocked him over. "I thought he'd kill you."

As the Texas Department of Public Safety swooped in with guns drawn, Ben lowered his weapon and gathered Kate in his arms, his hands weaving through her hair. He inhaled the scent of her shampoo, a huge weight lifting from his shoulders. "I wasn't too late."

She laughed and captured his face between her palms. "No, you weren't. And you saved more than me." She grabbed his hand and dragged him toward the barn.

The lawmen stepped in front of her, blocking her way.

Hank Derringer appeared beside the lawmen. "It's okay, they're the good guys." He swept past the men in uniform and stuck out his hand to Kate. "I apologize for not coming sooner. I'm Hank Derringer. And you're Kate. You have your father's eyes."

"I know." Kate smiled. "Your timing was good. And thanks for assigning this cowboy. I wouldn't be here shaking your hand without him."

"I knew he was the right man for the job." The older man winked at Ben. "Convincing him was the hard part."

"I'm convinced and glad you put me up to it." Ben touched a finger to Kate's cheek.

"You're not done yet." Kate took his hand and resumed her march toward the barn. "There are people in that barn."

As the words left her mouth, women and young girls peeked around the edge of the open doorway with dirt-streaked faces.

"We found them." Kate smiled up at Ben. "You're a hero. You saved these people."

"No, you did. I just came as backup." He hugged her to him and swung her off the ground. When he set her on her feet, he took her hand in his. "Let's go home."

Kate's smile faded. "I'd love to, but now that the bad guys are caught, you don't have to stay."

"The hell I don't." He slipped an arm around her and

walked toward the Mustang. "I know a little girl who'd miss me, even if her mother won't."

She batted his arm with a light pat. "You're growing on me, cowboy. Given time…who knows…a woman could fall in love with a man like you."

He stopped and turned to face her, cupping her cheeks in his palms. "That's what I'm counting on." Then he kissed her.

Epilogue

Kate sat with Ben on the porch swing, Lily between them, holding a very wiggly Pickles. The sun was setting on the horizon after a hard day's work on the ranch.

"Eddy and I got all the cattle rounded up and accounted for," Ben said, his hand twirling through a strand of Kate's hair.

Kate relaxed for the first time in a long time, content with her life and the direction it was going. "Think we'll have any more trouble with traffickers on the Flying K?"

"With the information Hank pulled off the flash drive, the Border Protection officers rounded up the gang of coyotes on this side of the border and the Mexican authorities claim they did the same on their side. I reckon they won't be hauling people across your spread anymore. You'll be happy to know that the women and girls found in the barn have been returned to their homes."

Pickles leaped from Lily's lap and scrambled across the porch.

Lily squealed and shot after him.

Ben scooted closer, pulling Kate into his arms.

Kate snuggled against him, pulling one foot up beneath her. "Did my father list the name of the kingpin on the U.S. side of the border?"

Ben shook his head. "No. But he left notes that he'd been working on. Hank will follow up on those. He's keeping the information close to his chest because your father mentioned a leak in our government."

Kate sighed. "At least they cleaned up around here, for now."

"You and Lily should be okay here on the Flying K."

Kate sat up straight and gave Ben a crooked smile. "That reminds me. I had some good news today."

"Did you stop by county records?"

"Yes, I did. The taxes were all paid up. The sheriff was just trying to scare me off the land so that Sanders's trafficking operation would go undiscovered and unimpeded. That's good news, but not *the* news."

Ben turned to her, his eyes narrowing. "What is it, then?"

"My father's attorney called. Seems the package I received in Houston wasn't all that my father left me. The attorney's been busy collecting all my father's bank information and sent me a detailed listing of the money my father had put away."

"Drug money?" Ben asked.

"That was my first thought. I wouldn't want any of that, not when people die every day in that business." Kate leaned into Ben, resting her head on his shoulder. "He received a salary from the FBI for his work with them and he set it all aside. Not to mention the FBI also carried a life insurance policy on him and I was named the beneficiary."

"Enough to get the ranch up and running?"

"More than enough." Kate tipped her toe on the porch, setting the swing in motion. "If I manage it well, Lily and I won't have to worry about money ever again."

Ben hugged her to him. "I know you were worried. I'm glad it's working out for you. You and Lily deserve to be happy."

She backed away enough to stare up into his eyes. "The point is…I can afford to hire ranch hands. You can continue working for Hank if you like."

Ben frowned. "Trying to get rid of me?"

"No, but I know deep down you're a cop and fighting for justice is what you do best. If working for Hank is what you want, then Lily and I will be here for you when you're not out on assignment."

Ben shook his head. "You're amazing. I think you know me better than I know myself."

She shrugged. "You're a good man, Ben Harding."

He leaned back and drew her against him. "And to think I didn't want this job in the first place."

Kate smiled up at him. "So what's keeping you?" She pressed a kiss to his lips.

"That, for one." Ben captured her face in his hands and deepened the kiss. "I never thought I could love another woman as much as my first wife." He paused, looking down at her. "I was right."

Her heart squeezing tightly, Kate's smile drifted downward. "What do you mean? You don't like us?"

"On the contrary. I love you more than I could imagine ever loving any woman." He brushed a kiss to the tip of her nose. "You're brave."

"Not where snakes are concerned," she argued.

"You're resourceful." He kissed her right cheek.

"A girl has to be, to get by these days." Kate's blood thickened, spreading warmth slowly across her body.

"And you make a great mother to Lily." He kissed her left cheek.

Kate laughed, her chest swelling with emotion. "What's not to love about Lily?" She clasped his cheeks between her palms. "Get to the point, cowboy."

"I think I'm going to love you for a very long time...if you'll let me."

"I'm counting on it, cowboy." Kate sealed her promise with a kiss.

* * * * *

REQUEST YOUR FREE BOOKS!
2 FREE NOVELS PLUS 2 FREE GIFTS!

HARLEQUIN

INTRIGUE

BREATHTAKING ROMANTIC SUSPENSE

YES! Please send me 2 FREE Harlequin Intrigue® novels and my 2 FREE gifts (gifts are worth about $10). After receiving them, if I don't wish to receive any more books, I can return the shipping statement marked "cancel." If I don't cancel, I will receive 6 brand-new novels every month and be billed just $4.74 per book in the U.S. or $5.24 per book in Canada. That's a savings of at least 14% off the cover price! It's quite a bargain! Shipping and handling is just 50¢ per book in the U.S. and 75¢ per book in Canada.* I understand that accepting the 2 free books and gifts places me under no obligation to buy anything. I can always return a shipment and cancel at any time. Even if I never buy another book, the two free books and gifts are mine to keep forever.

182/382 HDN F42N

Name _____ (PLEASE PRINT) _____

Address _____ Apt. # _____

City _____ State/Prov. _____ Zip/Postal Code _____

Signature (if under 18, a parent or guardian must sign)

Mail to the **Harlequin® Reader Service:**
IN U.S.A.: P.O. Box 1867, Buffalo, NY 14240-1867
IN CANADA: P.O. Box 609, Fort Erie, Ontario L2A 5X3
Are you a subscriber to Harlequin Intrigue books
and want to receive the larger-print edition?
Call 1-800-873-8635 or visit www.ReaderService.com.

* Terms and prices subject to change without notice. Prices do not include applicable taxes. Sales tax applicable in N.Y. Canadian residents will be charged applicable taxes. Offer not valid in Quebec. This offer is limited to one order per household. Not valid for current subscribers to Harlequin Intrigue books. All orders subject to credit approval. Credit or debit balances in a customer's account(s) may be offset by any other outstanding balance owed by or to the customer. Please allow 4 to 6 weeks for delivery. Offer available while quantities last.

Your Privacy—The Harlequin® Reader Service is committed to protecting your privacy. Our Privacy Policy is available online at www.ReaderService.com or upon request from the Harlequin Reader Service.

We make a portion of our mailing list available to reputable third parties that offer products we believe may interest you. If you prefer that we not exchange your name with third parties, or if you wish to clarify or modify your communication preferences, please visit us at www.ReaderService.com/consumerchoice or write to us at Harlequin Reader Service Preference Service, P.O. Box 9062, Buffalo, NY 14269. Include your complete name and address.

HI13R

Zach staggered back. The force with which the woman hit him knocked him back several steps before he could get his balance. He wrapped his arm around her automatically, steadying her as her knees buckled and she slipped toward the floor.

"Please, help me," she sobbed.

"What's wrong?" He scooped her into his arms and carried her through the open French doors into his bedroom and laid her on the bed.

Boots clattered on the wooden slats of the porch, and more came running down the hallway. Two of Hank's security guards burst into Zach's room through the French doors at the same time Hank entered from the hallway.

The security guards stood with guns drawn, their black-clad bodies looking more like ninjas than billionaire bodyguards.

"It's okay, I have everything under control," Zach said. Though he doubted seriously he had anything under control. He had no idea who this woman was or what she'd meant by *help me.*

Hank burst through the bedroom door, his face drawn in tense lines. "What's going on? I heard the sound of an engine outside and shouting coming from this side of the house." He glanced at Zach's bed and the woman stirring against the comforter. "What do we have here?"

She pushed to a sitting position and blinked up at Zach. "Where am I?"

"You're on the Raging Bull Ranch."

"Oh, dear God." She pushed to the edge of the bed and tried to stand. "I have to get back. They have her. Oh, sweet Jesus, they have Tracie."

Zach slipped an arm around her waist and pulled her to him to keep her from falling flat on her face again. "Where do you have to get back to? And who's Tracie?"

"Tracie's my twin. We were leading a hunting party on the Big Elk. They shot, she fell, now they have her." The woman grabbed Zach's shirt with both fists. "You have to help her."

"You're not making sense. Slow down, take a deep breath and start over."

"We don't have time!" The woman pushed away from Zach and raced for the French doors. "We have to get back before they kill her." She stumbled over a throw rug and hit the hardwood floor on her knees. "I shouldn't have left her." She buried her face in her hands and sobbed.

Zach stared at the woman, a flash of memory anchoring his feet to the floor.

Don't miss the second book in the
COVERT COWBOYS, INC. *series, TAKING AIM by Elle James.*

Available July 23, only from Harlequin Intrigue.

HIEXP0813